deki-san

Other Books by Tony Seton

Paradise Pond
The Francie Levillard Mysteries - Vol. One Through Six
Selected Writings
Jennifer
Trinidad Head
Just Imagine
The Autobiography of John Dough, Gigolo
Silver Lining
Mayhem
The Omega Crystal
Truth Be Told
The Quality Interview / Getting it Right on Both Sides of the Mic
From Terror to Triumph / the Herma Smith Curtis Story
Don't Mess with the Press –
How to Write, Produce, and Report Quality Television News
Right Car, Right Price

Other books from Seton Publishing

From Hell to Hail Mary - A Cop's Story - Frank DiPaola
From Colored Town to Pebble Beach /
The Story of the Singing Sheriff - Pat DuVal
The Early Troubles - Gerard Rose
The Boy Captain - Gerard Rose
Bless Me Father - Gerard Rose
For I Have Sinned - Gerard Rose
Red Smith in LA Noir - David Jones
The Shadow Candidate - Rich Robinson
Hustle is Heaven - Duncan Matteson
Vision for a Healthy California - Bill Monning
Three Lives of a Warrior - Phil Butler
Live Better Longer - Hugh Wilson
Green-Lighting Your Future –
How You Can Manifest the Perfect Life - John Koeberer

deki-san

by Tony Seton

September 2014

Carmel, California

This story is pure fiction – ideas snatched from headlines and whole cloth – and massaged by imagination and driven fingers. There is no correlation to either real people or events.

deki-san

All Rights Reserved

© 2014 by Tony Seton

ISBN-13: 978-1500994686
ISBN-10: 1500994685

Printed in the United States of America

Author's Note

I first took pen to paper with *Deki-san* when I was living in Chicago more than twenty years ago. Back then I wrote the first forty pages. I didn't know where the story was going. I never do. I eschew outlines and merely start typing. What I see on the screen drives the plot, fashions the characters, and commands my further attention.

Last month I returned to *Deki-san* and discovered that while I liked where it was headed, the book needed considerable work. The world is a very different place from where it was when I started. For instance, computers and smartphones are ubiquitous today. On a broader level, the book speaks of problems we weren't confronting then and which have worsened since.

What's also changed is that we are expanding our awareness of the human powers of perception. We are raising our levels of consciousness as well as the inherent competencies that come with greater awareness. This is a critical shift because we are acquiring an important understanding of our situation, and the skills we will need to fix and replace what's fallen into disrepair.

Yes, *Deki-san* is a novel, but a lot of the intuitive and conscious thought processes discussed in these pages has been framed by real experience.

While Francie LeVillard, the finest consulting detective since Sherlock Holmes, and her spook sidekick, Ariane Chevasse, play significant roles in this story, this not a *Francie LeVillard Mystery*. However, another volume of her stories is in the works.

So turn the page and meet journalist Cody Howard, and his amazingly plugged-in neighbor, *Deki-san*.

Thanks to Denise Swenson for proofreading this book.

Tony Seton
Carmel, California

deki-san

Preface

The bullet had left the gun. One-hundred fifty-eight grains of steel-jacketed lead hurtled toward the center of Cody Howard's chest at a speed designed to stop a moving target at a hundred yards in a fraction of a second. But as he stood only fifteen feet from the muzzle of the gun, the bullet was on track to strike its target in less time than it took to blink.

He didn't blink, but he did see the bullet – a black hole in the center of a sun that was the muzzle flash. It didn't take any time for his mind to register what his eyes saw, and to understand the future it dictated. He shouldn't have even had time to think "good-bye" but he did. Because of the flash of blue, the same color as Roy Deki's shirt.

deki-san

I

Cody Howard had met Roy Deki months earlier on the day he moved into his new home on North Palm Drive in Carmel, on the other side of Highway One from the quaint village of Carmel-by-the-Sea. He had just finished his first week as a reporter for KMTY television; or Channel 13, as it was promoted so potential viewers could more easily find the station. The man had just appeared in the garden in front of the house next door while Cody was busy unloading his belongings from the rental truck.

The unloading didn't take much time. It wasn't a huge load as most reporters live light. At that point Cody noticed that the man in the garden had stopped his pulling weeds from around a colorful froth of Icelandic poppies. He was a smallish Japanese man of at least 70 years, kneeling with great posture on a straw mat. Cody waved his arm, offered the proverbial "Hihowyadoin Howzitgoin" to the stooped figure, and then turned to go into his new house. The little man had remained still, but seemed to acknowledge the greeting with his eyes, and perhaps the hint of an incline of his torso.

At the time, Cody presumed the man was the gardener for the people who actually lived next door. Had his reporter's mind been on the facts, he might have inferred a different connection since the house had a distinctive Asian appearance, with red lacquered bamboo-wood trimming the ivory stucco building. In fact, the man was "the people next door," though that didn't become clear until they actually met later that day. That meeting would evolve into a vital relationship, though of course Cody hadn't the slightest notion in that moment of the man's importance.

Having been brought up on the East Coast in an intellectual rather than spiritual household, he had never given any thought to such concepts as serendipity or large purpose. His mind never entertained the deeper question of why he had moved into the house he did, or that there might be any significance to the older Japanese man tending to the garden of the house next door. His mind just didn't work that way, yet.

On the outside, Cody could be described as not quite ruggedly-handsome, but with thoughtful brown eyes under a trim brown hair cut. He stood maybe an inch under six feet, and while he didn't exercise, nor did he over-indulge in his consumption of food or drink, and so was in good health. At least physically. A hard-boiled journalist with a Cartesian – read rationalist – view of life, it would take some instruction from his neighbor before Cody would begin to grok the concept of serendipity. That's when his life took a sharp turn towards a different reality.

That turn was about to begin. Cody was puttering around in the upstairs of his new digs when he heard a soon-to-be-familiar sound of his doorbell. He had heard the deep mellow sounds from the old pipes hanging in the front hall, but it didn't take him long to figure out the source. He popped down the stairs and headed to the front door. It was mid-May, and a comfortable late afternoon. He'd left the door open to air out the house. As he reached the entrance hall, he saw the gardener from next door.

Cody's first thoughts were, "What did I do wrong already that would get me in Dutch in the neighborhood?" and "Oh-oh, maybe this was some wounded veteran who didn't know the war was over." A reporter's mind throws a wide net over possibility. His two bits of speculation evaporated almost immediately when the man bowed and then brought from behind his back a large freshly-sweating brown bottle of Japanese beer and extended it to Cody.

"Sapporo," he said, with a trace of an accent that would be familiar to people who had seen *The Karate Kid* or similar fare.

"Oh. Yes. Mr. Sapporo, how nice," Cody said as he reached to accept the bottle.

The man then reached out his hand to shake Cody's. "Yes," he said, "The beer is Sapporo and it is for you. My name is Deki." He made another subtle but pronounced bow.

"Oh, Mr. Deki, excuse me, and thank you. How do you do?"

"Fine thank you, and how do you do?"

"Oh, well," Cody said, nodding over his shoulder toward the obvious, "getting moved in."

Deki obligingly looked around at the furniture and boxes that filled but didn't yet make the living room. "Yes, you are." His eyes came back to Cody and while the pupils remained fixed, Cody said later that he could tell that he was being looked over. Or through.

"My name is Cody, Cody Howard."

Deki nodded.

"I saw you working in the garden over there. It's very beautiful." Actually, he hadn't really looked at the garden, merely taken it in on a scan as a lot of attractive colors and patterns.

"Thank you, Mr. Howard, I spend many hours of great joy in my garden."

That was when the reporter realized the man resided in the house.

"What brings you here, Mr. Howard? How is it that you are in this house?"

He asked in such a way – intensely but without force – that the reporter's mind offered that he was about to learn that the house was haunted, or that the last people who had lived there had disappeared, and that he, the new owner, would find them in the basement. These thoughts dissipated immediately when logic returned and he realized that the question had a scope broader than mere residency.

"I just got transferred," Cody began to explain. "I work for Enlaw Broadcasting; they own Channel 13 here in Monterey and a couple of other stations. I was working for their station in Toledo – Ohio – and they decided they could make better use of my talents here."

"Was it a promotion?"

The question was a surprise from a stranger, but somehow not intrusive.

Cody chuckled. "They didn't see it that way, but I've wanted to live here all my life, since I first came out here as a child with my parents." He paused. He had suddenly realized that there was something of importance about this man. "Have you lived here long?" He gave a nod toward his house.

Deki smiled. "I built my house. In 1973. I used to listen to the Watergate Hearings on the radio between hammering and sawing."

"What a neat way to imprint a memory of such an important time." The reporter paused for a moment. "Yes. It was an extraordinary time."

"Yes, it was. You will have to come over and see the house that was built while history was being written."

It was a curious way of putting it, but at the time Cody attributed it to a cultural or language difference. Over the months, it would become obvious that Deki's English was significantly better than most people's, including, at times, the reporter's own. The man spoke softly and used an economy of words, but any confusion over his side of a conversation was usually generated in the mind of the listener.

"Thank you for the beer, Mr. Deki," Cody offered as his neighbor turned to leave, "and I'd like to take you up on the offer to see your house..." He shrugged in the direction of the chaos behind him, "...when I get a little settled."

Deki stopped on the front step and turned. He was perfectly backlit by the closing rays of the waning afternoon sun, creating an aura effect around his head and shoulders. "Yes," he acknowledged, "Tomorrow, at six." It was less of an invitation than a command.

He caught Cody in mid-shrug with his shoulders up around his ears. There was no schedule conflict, and only his naturally reticent nature would have had him say no automatically. Instead he nodded until his shoulders reached normal elevation, and then his lips and tongue confirmed: "Yes, thank you."

II

Cody spent the next day bringing a degree of order to his new home. Much of the physical effort had been matched parsing his thoughts about his first week at Channel 13. It had been a discouraging five days, in truth, giving him serious cause to consider his situation. At five-thirty he took a shower and put on some fresh clothes. He was glad for a break, to relax and get to know his neighbor, and to learn about his new community. As it turned out, Cody did most of the talking.

"But why are you here?" Roy Deki repeated, not looking as though he were being denied an answer but still curious. Cody thought he had laid it all out for him in the first hour of the evening in his neighbor's spacious living room, beautifully appointed in a low-key way with classic Japanese prints on the wall and impeccably groomed bonsai plants around the room. For the briefest moment he thought perhaps his neighbor simply didn't understand what he had explained, but intuitively the reporter knew that the man was looking for something larger.

But Cody's intuitive side didn't have a chair at the table of his mind, except in dire emergencies. He hadn't read Jung, Einstein, or Dawkins, he didn't know about the anima and animus or the Tao, so he didn't know how he would benefit from listening with more than his ears. As a result, the repetition of Deki's question, now for the third or fourth time, pushed him out of his comfort zone.

But he did have the sense to broaden his explanation, at least on his own terms. He told Deki how three years earlier – to the day, as it happened – he'd been covering the arrival of more Marines in Kandahar for the network. After ten days of being up virtually all night, taking care of the evening producers and the morning show needs, the strain had taken its toll. The people at the network office hadn't a clue what it was like to be in a war zone 8,000 miles and ten time zones away.

Compounding his fatigue was his distress about how the network – not only his but the competition as well, and especially the cables – were covering the story. There was too much rah-rah about the 30,000 additional troops of Obama's surge, as if they would really change anything in "The Graveyard of Empires." The United States would follow the Soviets and the British down the costly path of defeat, leaving Afghanistan in as bad a mess as it was before Americans plunked down a trillion-plus dollars and thousands of lives in an impossible effort to accomplish...to accomplish what?

No one had an answer to that; not the politicians nor the media pundits. The obscenity of the situation as he saw it, together with the stress, ultimately freed Cody to say what he thought in a conversation with a field producer. His words were later relayed to a network mucky-muck in New York. Politics being what they were at the network, Cody's days there were numbered. So when it came time to be rotated back to the States, he decided to take a leave of absence and stay in-country, signing up for a six-week stint to help United Nations peacekeepers.

"That was three years ago today," he repeated, thinking back wistfully; his emotions again going raw. They were sitting together on a large couch, sipping plum wine.

"And then, how was it that you came here?"

Cody thought for a moment and continued, "Well, my timing wasn't terrific. And it wasn't really altruistic. I didn't think I could sleep back home if I left just there then. I wasn't going to make it my life's work, but it was what I needed to do at the time. Or so I thought, or hoped. But it turned out one of the local war lords wanted to make a point, so he accused me and another U.N. worker of being CIA operatives."

"And were you?"

"No," Cody replied, startled that he might be suspected of such a thing. "That would have been the furthest thing from my mind. It was just the Taliban messing with the only people who were really helping the people there."

"And so you left Afghanistan."

"Yeah," Cody remembered fondly, a smile rising on his face. "The State Department flew us out on a chartered jet. Very plush, great trip." He laughed as he recalled, "One of the self-important minions said he thought we should be billed for the flight – something like fifteen thousand each – but someone higher up nixed the idea when they realized how it would look to rescue Americans and then bill them for the rescue." He shook his head. "The same thing happened after Grenada, when they pulled out the medical school students. They were going to charge them for the flight to New York. You'd think they would have learned."

"Anyway, about a week after I got back, it was clear that the network didn't see me as essential, and I needed to look elsewhere for employment. As luck would have it, someone from Enlaw had seen the coverage of my return and thought they could milk the publicity for some ratings. So they offered me a weekend anchor job at their station in Toledo. The pay wasn't great, but I got a four-year, no-cut contract and I thought, why not, so I went."

Cody took a deep breath. "Why not, indeed. The people at Enlaw are a bunch of narrow-minded Midwestern stiffs who picked quantity over quality every time. The bottom line was the only line. They decided everything on the basis of ratings and dollars."

"But you couldn't work with people like that?" Deki said strongly, and with a tinge of surprise that Cody would have been fooled.

The reporter nodded his agreement.

"But I still don't know why you are here."

The reporter was pretty sure that his neighbor had been following his story. He'd stretched it over three hours of plum wine and dinner – a very enjoyable evening, in fact; the easiest time he could remember – but he still hadn't answered Deki's question it seemed.

"I didn't explain that?" he ventured, more curious than defensive.

"No, Mr. Howard, you told me how you got here. What I want to know is why."

III

Three weeks earlier, Cody had flown out to Monterey to meet the Channel 13 news director and to find a place to live. The meeting had almost been enough to sour him on the move, but he liked Monterey and, frankly, had no other real options at the time. Plus, he'd dealt with broadcast bosses before and was somewhat inured to their inherent venality. But the news director at KTMY pushed his limits.

"Howard, just so there's no confusion about why you're here," Herb Burgess flicked out his words, "I didn't ask for you, I didn't need you, and I didn't want you." With his tongue, he rolled the wet stump of an unlit cigar from the right corner of his mouth to his left. That might have been the some total of his exercise program.

Burgess tipped the scales at over three hundred pounds, his skin was sallow, he was untidy in his dress, he emanated a musty odor, and he showed little interest in the news. How he had gotten, and held, the news director's position was a matter of dank speculation.

Cody resisted the desire to respond in kind.

Burgess' comments were of a type uttered by villains in the grade b movies that played overnight on the sci-fi channels. Yes, he reveled in the power in his little fiefdom – it was like a drug for him – and thus he shielded himself from those who might shine a little light in his dark corner with unwarranted authority and undue rudeness.

Cody had indeed been foisted upon Burgess. He had been "sent down" from Toledo, the number 47 market in terms of audience size, to Monterey, the number 125 market, because he "didn't fit in." In point of fact, he was bumped because management didn't want to hear his complaints that the station was merely regurgitating the gore of police wire rather than producing anything that looked like journalism.

Burgess' counterpart in Toledo was a gratuitous little pipsquirt who had made it big as a media consultant by raising the ratings for several Enlaw stations by formatting their news according to the if-it-bleeds-it-leads approach. His ratings success had provided him with the opportunity to try his own hands-on management of the Toledo station's newsroom.

It was fortune, or misfortune, Cody thought at the time, that he'd been bumping his way down the ladder from his lofty correspondent job at ABC network television news to anchoring in Toledo. He had come to the station preaching journalism but the television news biz was long sinking into the post-Cronkite mire of ratings-come-first. Cody had been struggling for three years when the former consultant-cum-news-director arrived, on his way up the ladder. A diminutive man, unfortunately if cosmically named Shrimpstein, he had no shame.

"You can call it what you'd like, Cody," Shrimpstein told Cody on the second day he had been at the station. He poked a dispropor-tionately long index finger at his soon-to-be departing anchor, "but our shows get the ratings. And management," he said, looking up at the ceiling in the direction of the corporate offices, "doesn't give a shit what the critics – or the employees, for that matter – say about the news, as long as the count's up."

When Cody opened his mouth to respond, Shrimpstein had opened his hand into a stop sign, "Save your breath. We can have this conversation now or we can have it later. You hate everything I stand for, and I could care less. I decide who I work with, and you're not one of them."

Cody still had a year and five weeks left on the contract that his network experience had given him the clout to negotiate, and Enlaw was not the type of company to waste money by paying him off; though they had offered him the five weeks severance if he'd quit. Then they schemed and plotted and figured the best way to punish him was to send him down to their Monterey station.

"You've got to be kidding," he demanded of the corporate human relations VP who had the duty, and he thought, perverse pleasure, to tell him of the demotion.

"It's going to be an expensive move," Cody threatened.

"We'll pay for the move and give you ten for dislocation."

"Ten grand? What are you talking about? It's a whole different climate, I have to find a place to live, get my dog out there..." He let it trail off since, after all, he didn't have a dog.

"Ten is quite enough, Mr. Howard."

And actually it had been, at least for the move. But it wasn't nearly enough to wash down the bile that rose from the "welcoming" lecture from Burgess. Burgess tapped his head, and railed on. "I didn't get this job by sitting on my ass, Howard. I keep my ear to the ground, and nothing gets beyond me." The self-satisfied grunt added unneeded punctuation to his comment.

"I don't know who you fucked to get out here," he said, making clear how little he really understood of corporate politics, "but this is my shop and I decide what goes on, from the color of the paper in the bathroom to the weather forecast." He raised his eyebrows as if to underscore the last point.

"We got a year here together, and I don't intend to speak with you again until the day I hand you your last paycheck. In the meantime you do what Belotti tells you. Do we understand each other?"

Cody nodded blankly, mollified by a thought deep down that someday he would leave this hideous pretense of a human being in a heap. He left the news director's office quickly and headed for the newsroom. He had saved three months of sick days from his previous years with Enlaw, and he knew that they would be happy to see him on his way when he left in nine months. He could hang on that long, he thought; probably.

Nick Belotti was the assistant news director and the assignment manager and the news producer. He liked his job(s) and the authority they gave him over others, meaning the small news staff, and he would shine whatever shoes he had to keep the titles, meaning Burgess'. Belotti couldn't have looked more different from his boss, with a small frame and of average height, for which he thought he was compensating by wearing cowboy boots with two-inch heels. His face was thin and dark, and his forehead stretched to a high hairline that was little more than a comb-over.

Cody would quickly learn that Belotti's idea of news was whatever kept Burgess happy, or at least quiet. And Burgess was watching. Within ten seconds of the end of the early evening newscast, the special red "hot line" telephone on the producer's console would flash and Belotti would answer it in his own flash. Burgess would bark through the phone a letter grade rating the show, and then immediately slam down the instrument.

Belotti believed that Burgess didn't stay on the phone longer because he was demonstrating his economy of command control, but the truth was that Burgess simply detested Belotti and didn't want to talk to him. The grading of the shows was more to frighten the underling and keep him in line. Generally the grades hovered between C-minus and C-plus. A "B" would have brought Belotti as close to arousal as he'd ever been in his thirty years. Burgess knew an "A" would be fatal, but he didn't rule it out.

Of the two days Cody Howard spent in Monterey to check in with his new station and to find a roof, only a few minutes were wasted at the station. The rest of the time he spent driving around with a real estate agent looking for a new home. In the back of his mind, he knew that he wanted to live here after he left Channel 13, but he didn't want to come to grips with the if of "life after KMTY" at the moment. However, he did have to grapple with the issue of renting versus buying. Initially he planned to buy, that is, until he saw what his money could buy.

"You could buy," said the agent, Sherri Elm, who was sorting out the elements of her salad with her fork while she helped her client close the gap between his hopes and reality, realty-wise, "but you're going to have to lower your expectations on the size and location." A shortish, slightly overweight, middle-aged woman, she was comfortably nondescript in both her appearance and demeanor. Her husband made good money, and their children were out of the house. Real estate was perfect for her kind of gravity.

She had delivered the news about purchasing power on the Monterey Peninsula enough times in her career, finding that most people had taken it personally, feeling that they weren't worthy, or worth enough, and had then evaporated to another agent.

Sherri and Cody were sitting outside at The Clock restaurant, an institution in Monterey. It had a lot of charm, and was usually busy with locals who knew from regular experience that the food was decent-to-good and the prices were sub-tourist. At night, the place was mostly frequented my single men, but at lunchtime, many of its clientele came over from nearby Monterey Peninsula College and an assortment of neighborhood insurance, brokerage, and financial businesses that made up the majority of the non-tourist industry on The Peninsula.

"When you say lower my expectations," he asked, not thinking in any such terms of an insult, "what are we talking about?"

"Something cozy..."

"Small?"

"Quaint..."

"Old?"

"With a lot of charm..."

"Out-dated plumbing and wiring?"

"You understand," she confirmed with relieved sigh.

They spent much of the afternoon and the next day checking out the small, quaint, charming, and cheap that folded neatly into a folder he could toss into a trash can. After meeting the Channel 13 management, watching what they purported to be a newscast, and seeing the price of housing, Cody's early optimism over the move was fading with the afternoon sun.

"There are plenty of rentals, Mr. Howard," Sherri Elm told him as they parted shortly before he left for his flight back east. "If I don't find anything for you."

But then two days later she called. "Mr. Howard, I found your house."

There was such certainty – and delighted surprise – in her voice that he had no doubt that she was right. Suddenly the fog that hugged the central California coast and had accompanied his mood back to Ohio began to lift. She gave him the particulars about the house and then said, "I'll email you the pictures from the MLS book. It's vacant, an estate sale. I talked with the attorney who's handling probate. He says he's willing to let you move in before closing."

"It sounds ideal. How much is it?"

There was silence on the line. "They're asking ten thousand below what you said you were willing to pay."

Apprehension grabbed his gut; it couldn't be that good. "Let's see the photos and I'll give you a ring back."

Minutes later he was back to her. "Sherri, I think you're right. That's my house. You've found it." A small one-plus-story bungalow with two bedrooms, the wiring and plumbing had been updated, along with the kitchen and the roof. The price was right, and there was something else...a feeling that this was perfect for him.

The paperwork was FedEx'd back and forth, and his savings account collapsed to almost nil, but now he had a good feeling about the move to Monterey. Before he had been attracted to the geography and the climate; now, for the first time, he had a personal attachment to his future and it would be in his own home.

IV

Cody left Toledo in his 2012 maroon Camry for Monterey on the morning of the second Wednesday of May. He anticipated a fairly comfortable trip, most of it on Interstate 80, with his arrival on Saturday afternoon. Anticipating it would take him only four days, that would give him an extra day if he decided he needed to stop somewhere, or to relax for a day when he got there, and start work that Monday.

"Howard!" Belotti hurled the name as an invective across the fittingly-shabby newsroom only minutes after the new reporter had day-one deposited his few personal effects in the five-by-five cubicle that would serve as an office for the however-many-weeks-and-counting remained.

A green metal desk with a scratched Formica top took up half the space, reaching from the back wall to the front of the cubicle. Scratched might be the wrong word, he thought, reading a dictionary-worth of scatology that had been carved and penned into the top. Dates, too.

"Yessir," he answered, without thinking, and automatically sent word to his legs to follow the sound across the newsroom. Belotti's own desk was not much newer and probably only slightly larger, but he'd positioned it so that his back was to the wall as he faced out to the newsroom and the six reporters' cubicles.

Smart, Cody thought, he must have heard about Wild Bill Hickock. In two steps he was in front of his desk, trying his darndest to hide his thoughts and at the same time keep an open mind.

"Baptism by fire," Belotti half-sneered, "I want you to go down to Soledad. Seems some prisoners didn't feel they were secure enough so they grabbed a couple of guards and barricaded themselves in the library down there." He pointed at the door, and then with a faux touch of finality, looked back down at his desk.

Something told Cody not to ask, and sure enough, following his newsman's nose, he discovered that his obvious questions were just outside the newsroom door. A Channel 13 newscar was idling, and at the wheel was a taller than average, dark woman wearing trooper sunglasses and a patient smile.

"Howell?"

He thought to correct her then but waited until he was sitting next to her in the front seat of the car.

"Cody, Cody Howard," he told her as she shifted the car into gear.

"Okay, Cody, I'm Felice Inez. Shooter. Belotti never gets anything right." She snatched a quick glance for his reaction as she checked the traffic and then drove out onto Garden Road, heading east.

He allowed the left corner of his mouth to register an upward tick toward a smile. "How do ya do, Felice. He said something about a prison disturbance at Soledad?"

"Yeah, that's right. Soledad's 'bout an hour away. It could be over before we get there."

"'Baptism by fire' he called it."

"Oh, yeah, well, it could be something," she allowed, "'specially if they took hostages."

"That's what he said."

Felice fiddled with the frequency knob on the car radio and brought the microphone to her mouth, "Monterey Sheriff, this is Channel 13 car three. Come in." She clicked off the key, and in a moment a voice crackled back through the speaker beneath the dash.

"Monterey Sheriff, this is Hank. What's up, pretty lady?"

"Knock off that chit-chat, Hank. I got company."

"What? The new guy bounced down from Toledo?"

"Small town," Cody said, not nearly under his breath.

"Hey, Hank, he could hear that." She took advantage of the traffic light to give her new colleague a good looking-over, smiled resignedly at Cody and reported, "but I don't think you hurt his feelings."

"Welcome, dude," he continued. "What's up, Felice?"

"Hey, Hank, what's going down at Soledad this time?"

"Aah, Felice, they got a cute young thing like you going down there with all those Hispanics?" He dragged out each syllable.

"You know the score, Hank. They might need someone who can speak Spanish to mediate."

There was a chuckle at the other end. "Yes, indeed, they may need you today, pretty lady." The radio crackled off and then the voice returned. "The latest just off the police wire – hey, you think you could get me an audition? I got a great voice for anchoring – the latest is that they got nine or ten guys from B wing holding two guards in the library."

Cody noticed her eyes narrowed slightly when she heard "B wing."

"Whadda they want? More days off."

"Better food. Color TV. More yard time."

"It's good to want," Cody commented quietly enough not to be heard at the sheriff's office. It earned him another look.

"Thanks, Hank. Call us if you hear anything?"

"Sure thing, Felice."

"Will he?" Cody asked, surprised that the news folks might expect that kind of support from the authorities.

"Naw, it's just our way of signing off." She replaced the microphone in the holder.

"You know about Soledad?" she asked, her eyes on the two-lane road that would take them to Salinas and then to the highway south to Soledad.

"Not much. Medium security state pen. Sirhan Sirhan is there."

"He was. They moved him around. He's down in San Diego. But what you need to know if you're gonna be around is that it's basically the headquarters for two Mexican cartels that were being run out of LA. The bosses are doing time there, but they still run things by phone and through their lawyers."

"If everything is so hunky-dory, why do they have riots?"

"One, this isn't their play, and two, it's B wing. B wing is the hospital wing, and where they keep the psychos."

"So the baptism by fire."

"Hey, man, you don't have to worry. They won't let you in anyway."

Under raised eyebrows he asked, "Just you? You go in to mediate?" He was half-joking, half-ignorant.

"No, no, no. Once I did it, over here in the Monterey lock-up where they had a couple of boys who didn't speak any English. I was over there getting my press pass and they needed someone to tell the boys they were surrounded and stuff." She dodged a dead raccoon in the road and continued, "But when I said they won't let you in, I mean they won't let the press in. Ever. Except when someone like the head of prisons is doing a tour to show how great the place is. Then they bribe or sedate any of the prisoners who outsiders might see.

He took the opportunity while she was explaining to get a longer look at her. Of course her roots, he didn't know how recent, were Hispanic; she had a slight accent. She was also attractive, but hard; maybe due to the circumstances. Her skin was brownish, her long black hair was held in place by a silver and turquoise clip. Probably a couple of years around thirty, five-seven, on the sturdy side of slim, she was dressed in a red plaid work shirt and worn jeans and cowboy boots.

"So you were in Toledo? You must be glad to be out here, huh?"

"Mostly, so far," he responded half-heartedly.

"Well, it's a great place to live, if you have money. The ocean, the mountains – it's very comfortable."

"How long have you been here?"

"I've been shooting for the station for ten years." She looked over at him and answered the unasked question. "I started when I was 19. They didn't have any women and needed to show some color, too, so they got me out of a photography class at MPC; that's the local two-year college."

"Do you still enjoy it, or is it just for the money?"

She turned sharply. "It stopped being interesting most of the time about five years ago. Now it's just occasionally interesting. And the money, the money is chit, except that it covers the bills and maybe a little more. The station is the pits. They don't care whether you shoot good pictures or not, just so they have something to put on the air. Or maybe I shouldn't tell you that, this being your first day and all."

"No, that's fine. I don't think it's a surprise."

"What got you into trouble with the Enlaws?"

It was his turn to look up quickly. "I thought I was hired to show the flag of journalism, but they just wanted the same old fires, murders, accidents. With some sex and scandals thrown in."

"Oh, boy are you in trouble," the woman chuckled.

"Why's that?"

"Well, here, you're lucky to get real stories like that. Mostly they jus' replay press conferences and do features on kids and animals. Things are real quiet on the Monterey Peninsula. The management doesn't like to upset the viewers, 'cause then the advertisers pull their commercials."

"Unless there's a prison riot?"

"Well, yeah, but mostly it's pretty quiet down there, too. The gangs who run the place do a pretty good job of keeping a lid on stuff that would attract outsiders. If there's trouble, it's usually the B-boys. No one can control them."

As they turned off of River Road onto Highway 101, Cody shared with her a little of his background, not to brag but to let her know that she was working with a professional. She seemed to have seen his résumé already, and the professional was all she needed to know.

She seemed reticent to share anymore of her feelings about Channel 13. Maybe she didn't know who he was personally, as in, if he might pass along what he heard from her. He understood that. She would come to find out that he was safe to confide in.

They left 101 and drove up to the main entrance at the prison, a functionally-cold cinder block shack that mirrored the giant prison fifty yards and miles of razor concertina wire ahead. A guard stood in the doorway of the shack, one hand holding up the doorjamb, the other resting on the blue steel butt of his automatic. He seemed to take an inordinately long time looking at Felice.

She held out her press credentials; the guard looked past her. "We're going to the PIO's office."

The guard stood for a further moment and then picked up the phone inside the shack, never looking away from the car. He spoke a few inaudible sentences, replaced the phone in the cradle, and waved her toward the gate which rose before them. Felice drove forward. The gate clanked shut ominously behind them, but Cody wasn't phased, at least not a lot.

Felice drove them around the side of the prison to a trailer umbilicalled to the main building by phone wires. A small sign on the side of the building next to the door said it was Press Information Office and Lieutenant H.C. Reed was in charge. Felice parked next to the set of four wooden steps that led to the door. She got out of the car and leaned her head back in the window.

"You don't have to come in. I'll just find out what's going on."

"If it wouldn't cramp your style, I'd like to come in," and he got out of the car before she might raise an objection. He knew she thought she was just doing him a favor, and that was nice, but he had a certain way of doing things and not covering the story wasn't one of them.

"Sure," she said, acknowledging his meaning as she led them into the trailer.

The inside was as charmless if not more functional than the Channel 13 newsroom. The furniture had likely been bought at the same military-refuse auction. Two people were working there, a very pregnant, very young woman who was obviously not very happy to be there, and a crisp man of about forty who must have just walked off the movie lot where he had auditioned for the role of "martinet." He was happy to be there. He rose from his chair when he saw Felice and a mask somewhere between fear and lust froze his features.

"Ah, Miss Inez, how good to see you again." He didn't offer his hand as she might have ignored it.

She replied, "This is Cody Howard. He's a new guy at our station."

"Hi, Howard," he oozed in the frat voice used to sell insurance to the elderly. "H-C Reed. You can call me 'lieutenant.' Welcome."

The reporter laughed and immediately – having had all too much necessary practice – converted it into a cough. It was important to know a joke when it wasn't meant as one.

"Ah, great, lieutenant, thank you."

"Where you from?"

"Ah, Toledo. Ohio."

"Sure, sure, know it well."

Not having even the slightest interest, Cody didn't ask how or why. "So what's the story here, lieutenant?"

"Story? No story here, Howard."

The dismissal in his voice couldn't have been more final if he were closing the door in their faces. The reporter shifted his stance slightly so he was a couple of inches further away from the man wearing the beige with dark blue trim uniform of the state Department of Corrections. Every crease was sharp. Cody took out his notebook.

"What was the story?"

"Howard, there is no story, was no story. No story."

Even though he knew in the moment what the story was – the real story of denial and cover-up – Cody put on a look that suggested he was slightly befuddled, showing it first to the photographer, then back at the PIO. "I was told that a number of prisoners had taken hostages."

"No hostages."

"Now, okay, but there were some guards taken hostage?"

"What I said was that there are no hostages."

"Were there before?" Cody persisted professionally, and raising some hackles of impatience with a slight reddening of the man's neck and face.

"Howard, nothing's going on here. I don't know how else to put it." He waved his hand at the emptiness in front of the trailer. "Don't you think there would be a whole fleet of newscars out here if there was something going on?"

"Was there any kind of disturbance at the prison this morning?"

"Disturbance? There was no disturbance here this morning. Everything's just fine. Everyone's where they should be. Except maybe you. There must be an important story out there that's waiting for you. There sure isn't one here."

"B wing?" the reporter tried. It elicited the slightest tightening of the muscles around the PIO's mouth.

"B wing? B wing? B wing what?"

Cody hesitated. The energy in the small room had shifted from uncooperative to frosty, but not to threatening. He wasn't even sure why he had pushed this far, but he knew clearly that it was time to go. He gave a sheepish laugh. "You must think I'm a complete idiot," he shook his head. "My first day on the job, and someone had the sense of humor to send me down here to cover a non-story."

The man didn't respond but remained silent, his face painted with a frozen smile.

Shaking his head, Cody put his notebook away. "Okay, I guess we can go," he said to the stone-faced photographer who was also his driver. She led the way to the door. "Thanks, Lieutenant," he said with a deniable hint of sarcasm, and they left the building. They didn't stop to talk but got into the car.

Wordlessly, Felice started the car and drove them back out to the main gate. It wasn't until they were outside the wire and on their way down the road to the highway that the tension began to melt away.

"You did good back there, Cody." She had the trace of a respectful smile on her lips. That and relief.

He was silent for a moment. "What septic tank did they suck him out of?" he wondered calmly aloud.

"I told you, the gangs run the prison. If they can keep us out, they do. The warden and the guards are the same. The staff, too. They get paid by the state but they follow the orders of the prisoners. Otherwise they're looking for work which they wouldn't find. Or worse."

"So why'd they send us down here? Is this Belotti's sense of humor or is he just an idiot or something?"

She clearly appreciated her new colleague's candor and didn't stop a smile from lifting her cheeks. "Belotti's an idiot, but he wouldn't waste the gas on a wild goose chase. He thought there was a real story. You know, one they couldn't cover up."

"And your friend at the sheriff's office knew about it."

"Oh, sure. They have their sources...probably a lawyer for one of the inmates who was involved in the disturbance. They called their lawyer for protection. You know, to let someone outside the prison know what's going on inside, so maybe he wouldn't get a knife in him." She looked over at Cody. "They can hide a lot at the prison, but not bodies. And if there are too many killings inside, the people whose relatives are in there get upset, and so when the noise level gets too high, then the state's gotta do something about it."

"Do something?"

"Yeah, you know, they shuffle some people around to other prisons or re-assign some administrators in Sacramento if it's a really big deal. But usually it stays the same. Maybe shift a problem warden to a different prison with different gangs but it's all the same."

"Like what the Catholic church did with their pedophile priests," he said thoughtfully without thinking and looked hurriedly at her to make sure that he hadn't offended her.

She nodded her head. "Just like that." She was quiet for a moment and then asked, "Didn't they do it that way back where you were in Ohio?"

He thought about it. "Maybe they just hid it better back there." He was silent, digesting. "Now what? Call in that there's no story."

She shook her head. "We can't reach the station 'til we get past the mountains." She nodded to the ridge on her left that stretched to the horizon. "About fifteen minutes 'til we get radio reception."

Cody looked at her and was about to suggest the obvious, using a cellphone, but she knew he didn't know and with a hard grin told him, "We don't use cellphones calling in. Burgess," she shook her head, "he said only to use the radio so that we have an audio record of all communications. You know, so in case someone sues?"

"Sues? Why?"

Felice shrugged. "It doesn't make a lot of sense, you know. I think it's more because it would be more work for the people at the office. Plus the company would have to pay for us to have cellphones."

"Efficiency be damned," the reporter observed laconically. He didn't have a taste for any further conversation at the moment.

His shooter read his mood. "Hey, ya wanna get something to eat?"

V

"So how was your first day?"

Cody choked off the truth and fled for refuge to humor. "Well, I'm lying here in my room at the Seaside Motel Five..."

"Motel Five? Don't you mean Motel Six?" posed the inquiring mind in Connecticut.

"Nope. There's a single twin bed and no linens. It's a five."

Her genuine laugh created a painful smile in his mind's eye. Beth Rosemont was truly concerned that he was so far away, so far out of reach, even though there was nothing she wanted to do about it. She hadn't, even when he was closer in Toledo. Though Cody couldn't blame her for not holding a torch for Northern Ohio.

"Actually, Beth, the first day wasn't too bad."

"Did they send you out on a story? Did you get on the air? Is the motel really that bad?"

"Yes. No. No. The motel is really pretty nice. It's owned by the same corporation that owns the television station, so they're putting me up here. Anyway, I expect to be in the house next weekend." He didn't tell her that the only reason the station put him up in The Seasider Motel was because the previous motel had gotten tired of trading out rooms for commercials that did nothing to increase business, and who could blame them.

Beth knew him well enough after almost two decades of their relationship to know that he would not paint a true picture of his new situation if it was terrible if he thought it might worry her. So naturally she was worried. She also knew there was no value in her worrying, and only indulged the feeling briefly.

"So Alex gets there Saturday with your stuff?"

"That's what he said. He's driving in from Toledo, stopping to see some of the country, he said. I told him I had the house starting Friday, but I was working so he should come the next day."

"What, they don't even give you a day off to unpack?"

For a long moment, he resisted the temptation to tell her what he honestly thought about his new situation, but instead he let the feelings subside and then he gently blew her off. "Not to worry, Beth. I'll be fine here. It really is beautiful. I can't wait 'til you can come out and I'll take you all over the place. Monterey, Carmel, Seventeen Mile Drive. Big Sur."

Unmollified but also not ready to fly across the country to see him, she came back, "Then I'll give you some time to learn your way around so you can give me a proper tour."

They left silent the issue of when that might be. A minute or two of irrelevant schmooze and Cody begged off. Beth could try to reach him if she wanted, though he would be out a lot of the time, working, and he would call her from the new house.

With excessive care, he replaced the phone rather than pulling it out of the wall and throwing it through the window as was his primitive inclination. "Somehow," he said almost aloud, "that woman pushed everyone of my buttons, mostly the wrong ones and at the wrong time." Again he thought of what his crazy Aunt Ruth used to tell him, at length, about kindred spirits – people who had known each other in past lives. Yeah, well...maybe and so what in this life?

In this lifetime, they had met in college, fallen in love, had terrific times, and fallen out of love. But unlike many of his past relationships, he had stayed in touch with her. He and Beth had gotten together, talked through their past highs and lows, and realized that they were not supposed to be lovers. They simply didn't feel a passionate need for one another. What might have been wasn't any more.

Maybe it was the distance – geographical and otherwise – that caused him to replace the longtime memories of Beth with the fresh memory of the day's events. Cody suddenly felt tired. He started playing back a mental tape of what had happened since he'd left this same bed some fifteen hours earlier, hoping that he would soon be drifting off. Ah, *to sleep perchance to dream.*

That morning after a breakfast of undercooked eggs and questionable ham, pulpless fruitade and black swill in a coffee mug, Cody had checked in with Burgess who grunted at him and then returned to his paperwork, and then with Belotti who said, "Yeah well..." and picked up a ringing phone on his desk. The reporter returned to his cubicle, thinking he might figure out how many days he would have to keep his mouth in check with them, but he had promised himself that he would wait at least until he had been there a week before he indulged in the math and set the timer.

His next recall was of Felice Inez; a nice lady, he thought. Street smart, hiding a heart. She was probably going to be more than a colleague. No, he wasn't thinking of anything amorous but a confidante maybe. After leaving the prison, they had retraced their route up Highway 101 to Spreckels, and on a back road over to Highway 68 which would take them to Monterey. Felice had pulled into the dirt parking lot of what looked more like a house than a restaurant. The small white adobe building had a dozen cars parked haphazardly in front, and there was a bright yellow ten-by-ten sign with the words "Toro Café" in red letters. The sign was bright enough to be a beacon for airplanes but it was inside that had attracted the customers, probably many of them repeats.

The interior design was equally arresting – contemporary *tourista* kitsch – and the food, Felice assured Cody, was *autentica*; he decided the word was Mexican for *spicy*. But it was very good, too, and he enjoyed her company as he listened and ate, and she talked. She was very generous with her commentary and open in what she had to say, considering how long she'd known him. Part of it was her own self-assurance, and the other part was that she'd seen enough to know that he was not a spy or a rat.

First she explained the management. Big Don ran the station. Big Don was Donald Centree II who was married to an Enlaw daughter and was listed as the President and General Manager of KMTY. It was really for corporate purposes only because with the Enlaw family if it wasn't blood it wasn't for sure. Centree has the authority to run the station the way he wanted, as long as he meets their profit goals. "And as long as he keeps his wife happy, of course," Felice added. "That was the most important."

She then proceeded to give the new reporter a low-down on the major players in the news department. It was a short list since the 125th market didn't require much of a staff, either in quality or quantity. The anchors and the reporters were fairly interchangeable, which was not the habit at most stations. Most stations hired anchors whom they could market as recognizable personalities to the community, building name recognition, an audience, and ratings.

But Channel 13 spent very little money on promotion, and to save even more, their reporters and anchors were all part of a team. They were paid the same salaries with the same meager benefits. Burgess considered this a pioneering new concept, but no one was fooled. It was his way of keeping salaries low.

Those reporters who wanted to get some anchor experience – and fresh videos for their resumes – had to do some sucking up to the news director. If they were successful, the fat man would send an e-mail to Belotti's computer where it would set off a little red light and small bell which would flash dully and ring atonally until Belotti typed in a special code to receive and acknowledge the latest confidential edict. Then a new face would be behind the anchor desk for a try-out. If he was better than the person he had replaced, he'd stay until someone else, adequately obsequious, got a shot. That said, the current anchors had held their positions unchallenged for almost a year, something near a station record.

Having been in town only for two days two weeks prior – to sign the papers and find a place to live – Cody hadn't had a real look at his professional circumstances. Big Don had brought him up to his office for all of ten minutes to welcome him before sending him off to look for housing. Now buried in Cody's soul, more deeply than ever, was the awareness that every time he been told "Glad to have you on board" he should have looked for a lifeboat.

In his motel that night and the next before he returned to Toledo to pack and close out with whoever deserved goodbyes, he'd watched the five and eleven o'clock newscasts. That was all the KMTY did. They didn't bother with news inserts into the network's morning show, and at noon they aired a syndicated cooking show. The early and late evening half-hours were little more than a nod to the FCC and did little to serve the community.

It was watching the news those two nights that gave Cody a feeling for the "team" of which he was becoming a member; albeit temporary and unwilling. Luckily, the first night he watched the show in his motel room alone with eight airline bottles of Smirnoff martinis, the gift of a friendly flight attendant who had recognized him as a celebrity but hadn't remembered why.

Cody had watched purposefully, registering the formatting of the stories, the anchor bridges, and the styles, strengths, and weaknesses of the other members of his "team." There were no strengths, and he only briefly thought of tracking the mispronunciations and flawed grammar because it would take too much effort. Instead, he dispelled his distress by tearing the tops off the Smirnoff bottles and pouring the contents down his throat. He was reminded that booze was overrated when it came to numbing the mind.

The newscasts were a jerky kaleidoscopic montage of graphic news footage from around the world, plus a cacophony of local leaders trying to sound important, all brought together by a few self-important reporters. It was something like the drive-thru at Carl's Junior on a Friday night. Hosting the newscasts were the two anchors, perched on a couple of high director's chairs sitting in the newsroom

Actually they weren't in the newsroom, which would have shown poorly. Instead, they were sitting in front of a colored flat, and a shot of a professional-looking newsroom – probably from another Enlaw affiliate – was "key'd" in behind them.

The anchor team, or current flavor, was Ron Ross and Lara Lee. Maybe because he connected the double-R name with Rolls-Royce, but Ross really thought a lot of himself. He had no reason to. His diction was weak, and inflection off. A viewer might wonder if he understood what he was reading.

Lara was an amiable young woman, and like the rest of the on-air "talent" at the station, in her mid-twenties. She had intended to be a hair colorist in Hollywood but discovered that her skin didn't get along with the chemicals. Her luck changed when she entered a beauty contest.

As Felice had explained to Cody, hiding little of her contempt, "She was queen of the Gilroy Garlic Festival. Big Don saw her in a news story I shot up there, and he had to meet her. He was real discreet, right? He comes down to the newsroom, puts the tape of the show in the machine, and tells Burgess to 'Find that girl and get her on the air before the competition discovers her!'"

"And Burgess performed?"

"Yeah, and you know the funny thing, Channel 8 over in Salinas, they were actually thinking of going after her, too."

Ron and Lara were the perfect team. Nothing got by them. In fact, nothing really reached them. Their large, incessantly vacuous smiles were genuine and engaging. Ask anyone at the Shady Woods Home for Nonagenarians, another Enlaw investment. Ron and Lara didn't garner much of an audience, other than tourists who didn't know better, or care about, the local news. But thank goodness for the tourists. As the Monterey Peninsula was a tourist mecca, Channel 13 drew enough of an audience to generate enough revenues to stay on the air. The locals, who had some use for the news, watched the competitor, the NBC affiliate in Salinas.

It wasn't that Ron and Lara didn't do a professional job of presenting the days events – they didn't – it was more important that they, and those who watched (often in bars with the sound turned down), didn't want their moods interrupted by reality. Symbiotically, it meant that the only companies that wanted to advertise on the station were those going after the tourists, e.g. restaurants, schlock shops, and entertainment venues. It was another reason that the locals wouldn't watch; they knew the advertisers already and would have nothing to do with them.

Cody and Felice ate for a while in silence, and then Cody asked, "Felice, not to be too personal, but aside from the money, is there anything keeping you at the station?"

She stopped chewing for a moment to give her full powers of concentration to the question. She began chewing again and soon the words followed. "You know, there's something about the news business that I really, I don't know, feel." She patted herself in the middle of the chest. "It's like sometimes we have a story on the air that I shot that may get people to act different. Maybe regular people, maybe politicians sometimes. That means something to me.

"But if you mean like at the station itself or anyone there, or would I go to Hollywood with a rich guy if he asked me...in a minute." She finished her tostada with a smile of knowing satisfaction. And as they walked out, she said to him, "It was good, right?"

"*Autentica*," he responded.

As they got into the car she handed him a roll of Tums. "For later. Real *autentica*."

VI

"Cody, ya been here what, a coupla hours, and you're already pissing off state officials," Belotti delivered the announcement to a newsroom in general when his new reporter walked in the door. As it happened in the early afternoon, the newsroom was empty except for the two of them; Felice was parking the newscar.

"I beg your pardon," Cody responded, wondering in the moment if this was the man's sense of humor.

"We got a call just after you left the prison. Seems you were," he paused to shuffle about for a piece of paper that was immediately in front of him on his desk and then read from : "'aggressive and rude' and you didn't know when to leave." Belotti put the slip of paper down and tried to look down at Cody while he was sitting at his desk and the reporter was standing in front of him.

"I don't know where you think you get off, being big city smart..."

"Toledo, big city? What an asshole!" Those were the subtitles that flashed across Cody's mind as he listened to Belotti while he showed him a poker face.

Suddenly the heat rose, "Listen, Belotti," he wasn't shouting but the tone of his voice pushed the man back in his chair, "I don't know who called you, but I categorically deny any 'aggressive' or 'rude' behavior. And as far as my departure, it was only because this was my first day that I didn't stay longer."

"Don't call him Belotti." The voice was icy smooth – even the teletype machines went quiet – but not belligerent. It belonged to Big Don who had come into the newsroom without notice. "Call him Nick or Mr. Belotti, but calling him by his last name cheapens our team image."

The instruction was addressed to Cody. Now he addressed them both. "What exactly is causing this argument, Nick?"

Belotti, not used to addressing the station manager personally sputtered out some "ums" and "ers" but wasn't able to get out a coherent thought. Cody took over.

"The discussion I was having with Nick," he said, emphasizing the name, "was over an assignment I had this morning."

"Oh, sending you out already, is he?" put in the station manager said to lighten the atmosphere. "Good. We want to make the most of you."

"Uh, huh..." Cody replied, realizing that the man was serious. "I went down to check out a report of a disturbance at Soledad, spent five minutes getting a total denial that anything had happened from the PIO." He thought to explain what the letters meant but didn't want to risk sound condescending. "I get back and am greeted by Nick here saying someone associated with the prison had called to complain that I was aggressive and rude, and that I wore out my welcome."

"I wouldn't expect that of you, Cody. Was there a misunderstanding of some sort?" Big Don asked.

The reporter felt like a child with a dense parent trying to arbitrate with a prevaricating sibling. With considerable effort, he stifled the compulsion to scream himself awake, and said evenly, "I didn't do anything of the sort, sir. I was perfectly civil, I was polite, and I got out of there before I should have. And what pisses me off, if you'll pardon my French, is that Nick made the presumption that I had done something wrong."

"Well, I can certainly see that you would be annoyed, Cody." He turned and look down at the stunned factotum seated before him, "Nick, I do see his point, don't you? I mean, he is on our team now." He gave Cody a wink, "And I think he needs to hear that from you."

Belotti's world had been turned on its head. He had never had to deal with a higher-up except for Burgess. He managed to jiggle his head is such a way that he indicated his concurrence.

"Good," said the station manager, turning back to the reporter. "Now Cody, was anyone else with you when this *alleged* incident occurred?"

"I was with him every second, Mr. Centree." Felice Inez had come into the newsroom just as the discussion had started and had heard everything. She stood in the doorway, slightly behind Belotti. Her voice provoked a swivel in the producer's neck that sounded like a shot.

"Hello, Miss Inez, how nice to see you again." Big Don smiled magnanimously at her. "I believe the last time must have been the awards banquet. You won that award, didn't you? Which one was it again?"

"Spot News, sir. Thank you for remembering."

"Yes, of course." He turned to Cody. "She's a real asset to the station."

Cody nodded. At that point he wouldn't have been surprised if Rod Serling had suddenly appeared.

"Now, Miss Inez," the station manager asked, "can you tell us please, if our new man here did anything that could have been deemed out of line?"

"Yeah," she almost spat out the word. "He didn't call Reed a lying asshole." She smiled coquettishly. "Pardon my Mexican."

Big Don wasn't a bit fazed; he ran a television station, after all. He nodded his pardon and then confirmed, "But otherwise Cody behaved quite the way we would want him to?"

Felice gave him a confident smile. "He was a perfect gentleman, Mr. Centree. He didn't say a thing that could be interpreted as 'aggressive' or 'rude.'" She drilled a look between Belotti's beady little eyes, "Nick, you sent him down there...what, to feed the lions?" She turned back to the station manager. "Sir, Reed's a lying jerk, always has been, always will be 'til they get a warden who's better than the one they've got, and he gets rid of him."

"Well, what really happened then, do we know?

"From what we learned, they had another mess-up in B wing down there, but wouldn't admit it. They'll probably be notifying a coupla families in a coupla days that there was an accident in the laundry or something. Closed caskets, extra funeral payments. Over and out."

"That would have been a good story. Too bad we were frozen out." Big Don clapped his hands together with finality, "I'd say that just about wraps it up for me. You found out what you needed to I trust, Mr. Belotti."

Belotti nodded a "yes" and followed with "Yessir" to the departing figure. Three pairs of eyes followed the station manager to the door where he briefly double-parked to wave goodbye, and then he disappeared.

Cody gave Belotti one of those special don't-fuck-with-me looks and nodded a sincere thanks to Felice before going to his cubicle. She followed him.

"Welcome to the world of Channel 13," she said, with a smile that showed her pleasure at having just prolonged his stay.

"Thanks, Felice...for sticking up for me."

"Hey, it was the truth. I wouldn't lie for anyone."

"Yeah, I didn't think you would. It's just that aside from you and me and," he nodded in the direction of the recently-departed station manager, "truth doesn't seem to have a high premium on it."

"Yeah, well, ya gotta be discriminating," she said with mock sternness, and showing a smile added, "you know, the right kind of discrimination."

He gave her a smile back.

Her voice tightened, "Hey, did you notice in the office?"

"You mean Reed's?"

"Yeah. The phone."

Suddenly he recalled what hadn't registered earlier; the flashing line button.

She clarified the point. "Someone was on hold the whole time we were there."

"Hmm. Was he waiting to speak to someone, or were they waiting to speak to him?"

"I don't know, but I'll tell you one thing. Something happened at Soledad today, and they didn't want anyone to know about it." With that she raised her eyebrows, then turned, and left Cody realizing how much he had yet to learn – about Channel 13, Felice Inez, and Soledad prison.

VII

Cody sat on the front step of his house the following Saturday morning waiting for his friend to pull up in the truck. Alex had called four hours earlier from Sacramento where he'd spent his final night on the road. Cody felt some nervousness over the size of the changes in his life. New job, new town, new geography, new climate, new people, new home. "New future," he said softly aloud.

He closed his eyes and took in a deep breath. His nose was filled with the soft pungency that wafted from the two big pines at the end of the block. Was there also a scent of salt in the air from the Pacific, only a couple of miles as the breeze flies, over the hill behind the pines? He suddenly felt very emotional. He well understood that a lot was happening with him, to him, in him. He didn't know what it was – churning, cleansing, preparing.

He did know that he felt better than he had since he could remember. His body felt looser, less rigid. He twisted himself around, feeling the many muscles he was stretching. Looking past the white clapboard walls through the open bleached oak door, he saw the bare wooden floors of the living/dining room, back to the small fireplace built into the corner. He smiled; he hadn't had a fireplace in his home since childhood.

He heard the truck coming up the hill before he saw it. The silver 14-footer trimmed with "U-Haul" orange meandered up the street in second gear, coming into sight around the corner, with Alex propped up in the driver's seat checking the house numbers for 308. He spotted Cody waving and pulled up in front of the house. The smile on his face as he looked at his friend's new home was a good review.

He jumped down and Cody gave him a big hug. Released, Alex walked past him up the two stairs, across the short porch and into the house. Cody followed him in and around as he walked through the living area and kitchen, and then upstairs to the bedrooms. It wasn't until they returned to the porch that he declared, "You did good, Cody, real good."

A contractor who did his own woodworkng, Alex Derwickey was very physical and in good shape. Though small, he man-handled the furniture from the truck into house with little effort. All of Cody's things – his furniture and the boxes that contained his life's possessions – were in their new places in only a few hours.

The two men sat on the front steps, enjoying the mid-afternoon sun and some beer and sandwiches Cody had picked up on to the way to the house that morning. Alex was driving back to Ohio, starting that afternoon. He was helping another friend moving East from Stockton. Cody repeated an invitation for his friend to stay over and leave in the morning.

"Gotta get back, Cody. The guys are going to finish two houses at the end of the month. I gotta go back and do a bannister and a mantle."

It wasn't really "gotta." It was what he wanted. Alex had been successful for years, and the time he spent on these custom projects were his special pleasure.

"Have to say, Cody, you got the better deal."

"Better than what?"

"Better than my friend Sally, who I'm moving to Akron. She's following her fiancé who's got a job at a tire factory."

"Management?" he asked hopefully for his friend.

"Yeah, but you know the economy."

"And it's Akron." They said it together.

"So Alex, did I do well enough that you're going to come visit?" he asked. Aside from this double favor for friends, Alex didn't travel far from Toledo. He genuinely liked it. Felt at home there. Cody now better understood what the feeling of "home" meant.

"Oh, don't know about that, Cody. You know me – never flown in an airplane."

He was not really proud of the fact, but held it up as a demarcation point of sorts. "Although I gotta say, I didn't know there was a place like this. I said that about Sacramento. It's nice, you know, lotsa space, and trees. But when I got off the highway at the coast, you know, where it comes down behind the dunes?"

"Just before you get to Ft. Ord."

"That's right. And then you see Monterey...." He patted Cody's knee. "Well, you might just see me again. I'm glad you found this." And getting up he said, "I know I won't have to worry about you."

"Just know that you've got a place to stay on the coast any time."

"Thanks, Cody. I just may take you up on the offer."

They hugged each other again, and Alex walked down to the truck. He checked the lock on the back door, and climbed up into the cab. He turned the truck around, waved and headed down the street. Cody watched him until the truck was out of sight, and then a little longer.

Alex and he had been friends for most of the time Cody had been in Toledo. He regretfully admitted to himself that it was unlikely he would ever see the man again, all good intentions and immediate emotion to the contrary. He could hear the grinding of the truck gears at the stop sign at the bottom of the hill, and in a short time, the engine sound, and his connection with Toledo, was gone.

VIII

The house was certainly a good reason to find work after his stint at KMTY, however long that was to be. As pleased as Cody obviously was at his new home, he didn't let on to Alex about how his professional life was panning out. So far, there were only a few valuable nuggets in a pan full of useless dirt.

On Tuesday, he found himself in that nether world between rookie and drone. He knew how to cover a news story better than the vast majority of reporters in print and broadcasting in the whole country, and he had a whole wall-full of awards, commendations, and trophies to prove it. These accolades were all packed away, because if you're good enough to earn 'em, you don't need to tell anyone about it. Not that it mattered to Cody, but it did – or should – to other people, especially those where he worked.

The trick for him at his last few jobs was that their definition of what was news wasn't what he had learned it to be, and what he continued to believe it was. For Cody, the Fourth Estate was not an industry but a calling. It's function was essential to the healthy working of the country. Regrettably, perhaps disastrously for the nation, business interests had taken over news and switched it from a critical information provider to an entertainment medium, fig-leafed with a pretension of reporting current events.

In most markets, news reporting had degenerated into blood-n'-sperm tabloid coverage. The dictum was to blend the newscasts in with the prime time schedule, with as much sex and violence as could be justified. But in a few markets, a number of stations had gone to the other extreme, reporting just "good" news. Lots of animals and children, flower shows, do-gooder programs, and press releases from local businesses, especially advertisers. Herb Burgess pandered to the business interests of The Peninsula in this way, programming for an audience that didn't want to get indigestion from watching the local news. As Cody didn't have a grasp on who were the players in this new state, region, and market, he was going to have to feel his way around for a while.

Cody knew that nearly fighting with Belotti on his first day on the job wasn't the kind of performance that was going to prolong his career, and so he was all set to play nice and forgiving when he walked into the newsroom the second day on the job. He was not prepared for the greeting he got from the man.

The little man hoisted himself to his feet and in a gruff, camaraderal tone said, "Nice job yesterday, Howard. You really held their feet to the fire." In light of the conversation of the afternoon before, the best Cody could do was to look appreciative of the strokes. He overcame the urge to remind Belotti, whose turnaround he regarded with suspicion, that the use of last names was not politic.

In a confused gesture of humility and false admiration, Belotti thrust out his hand. Reflexively the reporter took the small hand in his own and gave it a perfunctory shake. He felt that he had graduated, but he didn't know from what or to what. Belotti regained his seat. Wordlessly Cody turned toward his cubicle

"By the way, Cody, word from upstairs," said Belotti, nodding up toward executive-dom, "he wants you to spend the rest of the week going out with other members of the news team. You know, so you can get a feel for the territory."

"Okay, great," Cody answered noncommittally, discombobulated by the unexpected appearance of common sense.

"Today, I want you to go out with Lane."

As if on cue, that over-coiffed young man came down the hall from the washroom. Bubbling with that self-proselytizing energy that raises the gorge of any sound mind, Lane Headworthy, a tall, thin man wearing a plaid jacket over a striped tie of conflicting colors, was visibly lifted at the mention of his name. Seeing the direction in which Belotti was talking, he swerved and made a beeline for Cody. For the briefest, and humorous moment, Cody entertained himself with the thought about turning Alex around.

"Hi, Headworthy's the name, television's the game. Call me Lane."

"Lane. Lane Headworthy," Cody semi-gushed with an enthusiasm that raised a twitch above Belotti's right eye. "I saw you on television." And then, "You must be winning your game."

It was his tone of voice – effusive, excited, syrupy – that impressed his young colleague, since he clearly didn't get what Cody had meant.

"Hey, great. Thanks." He made a pseudo-athletic feint away, and pointed at Cody as though his hand was a gun. "Right on target."

"So where are we going today?" Cody felt the use of the word assignment might be too large for him. His real question was, "How was I going to get through this day?"

"Hey, Belotti, whaddya got for this crack team today?"

Belotti handed him an assignment sheet, and Headworthy led Cody out the door.

Cody wondered if he was being punished. Headworthy led them out to a rusty green Pontiac circa 1995 parked in the first stall. A young Asian man sat behind the wheel. Headworthy got in beside him and Cody opened the rear door. He tried to slide, and maybe he did, over what looked like a very unclean back seat. Someone had come up with the idea of covering up the springs in the original seats with orange-tinted lambskin throws – maybe ten years earlier.

They pulled away from the curb without introductions, Headworthy already in full-blown exposition on what Cody should know about the coverage strategy he had mapped out. It started with a plan for cut-aways. Cody made no attempt to interrupt the monologue, but instead noticed in the rear-view mirror the driver dividing his attention between the road and the new guy in the back seat.

Finding a nanosecond of pause in Headworthy's monologue, Cody jumped in like the pro he was. "Yo, Lane, come up for air." And when the man stopped talking, Cody asked, "Who's driving?" He didn't think it necessary to point, though he realized that pointing would have saved some time in developing a response.

"Oh, that's Fergarella. He's Filipino. Fergy the Filipino we call him.

Doesn't speak a word of English. He's our videographer today. Great guy."

As Headworthy went on, Cody saw out of the corner of his eye that while the Filipino might not speak English to this reporter, he probably understood plenty.

"Just point him in the direction of the shot you want and you've got it. And he's not a real stickler about when he eats. Which is fine." Headworthy thought for a moment and added, "I don't think he likes pizza."

Maintaining control of the flow for his own amusement, Cody asked, "Not to change the subject, but is Lane Headworthy your real name?"

After a longish hesitation, Headworthy launched into a new line.

"Actually, I was named after my father whose name was Lance, but the hospital spelled it wrong on the birth certificate, and my parents figured that my name was supposed to be Lane. Neat, huh? Go with the flow."

That was about as enlightening as the day got. Cody managed to get by with a short list of grunts and head-bobs, turning most of his attention to observing landmarks and asking questions mostly unrelated to what Lance's boy Lane was saying.

Ft. Ord was the destination. Today the local congressman and the state representatives were meeting with Defense Department officials to discuss what was going to happen to the remainder of what was once an important training base. Most of the land and some of the buildings had been turned over to a local agency, but there was a section that a developer had been eyeing for ten years for mixed use including low-income housing that the Pentagon had been sitting on for no apparent reason other than bureaucratic lethargy.

The DoD had called this meeting to share their vision, which, it turned out, was for the locals to buy back the land that the Army had confiscated decades earlier. Oh, except for a small section – the nicest property on the entire base, it turned out – that they would keep for top officer training and seminars. How nice for them.

Not for the locals. And for the first time in local memory, according to what Cody picked up from the conversations among other reporters covering the event, the Congressman, Mark Longe, blew his stack. Longe was a very bright fellow who rarely made headlines, even locally, except small ones well inside the paper, but this time he let it all out.

In a sound cut that made the air from San Francisco to Washington, Longe told the DoD officials, "You have poisoned the base with fuel dumps and unexploded bombs and shells, and now you want to sell us back our own land. Except for the best piece, which you will keep for yourselves? This will not happen!"

The sound cut played in Salinas, too, but not in Monterey. Well, to be accurate, the video played, but the audio was accidentally erased. Lane Headworthy could have cared less. "Hey, as they say, shit happens. The standupper looked good. I looked good. I sounded good. What do I care if the technicians screw up."

No question mark. It wasn't a question. Cody somehow managed to mask his ire, but the lack of distress in the Channel 13 newsroom at what had happened made it unequivocally clear that the situation was borderline irreparable. Curiously, though, that conclusion provided a sense of release and relief. Cody wasn't sure why, but he felt that there was another route for him; that when it came time to leave the station, he wouldn't be leaving the area. In fact, when he awakened the next morning, he felt very good about his future. He didn't know why, but he felt confident that he was on the right path.

Those good feelings were tried over the next three days, as Wednesday, Thursday and Friday were mostly the same in terms of the level of quality and effort he witnessed on the job. Lara Lee, the former garlic queen turned anchorwoman, covered the dedication of a new section of Fisherman's Wharf. She reported the story without mentioning significant cost overruns and a pollution problem that had yet to be diagnosed. But the Chamber of Commerce couldn't have asked for a better report.

Then there was the court hearing for the Seaside mayor picked up on a DUI. He was black as was most of Seaside, so Belotti dispatched Colleen O. Murphy, a black woman, to cover the story, and Cody went along. (Felice had filled in Cody about Colleen O. Murphy...how when she had first arrived at Channel 13, she had dyed red hair. Her explanation to everyone who asked about her dye-job, and to those who didn't even think to ask but were told anyway, was that she didn't want people to think of her as black. She asked that people call her "Red," but no one did. Most people called her "O." instead.)

There was nothing to the court hearing. The mayor's attorney complained that his client was the victim of racial profiling but the assistant district attorney was waiting for him. She noted that only 75% of the people stopped by police in the area were black while 80% of the populace was black. The judge glared at the mayor's attorney who whispered hurriedly with his client, which whispering produced a "no contest" plea, a fine, and community service. Murphy led her report with the racial profiling non-issue, and then did an artful walk-through of a senior citizen center noting that this was where the mayor would perform his community service.

And to cap off Cody's mind-arresting first week at KMTY, he went out with the sports editor, Buck Schotz, to cover the summer league try-outs of the ladies auxiliary softball team in Marina.

"I know you're dying to ask, so I'll tell ya," the sports editor offered, "Buck Schotz is my real name. No kidding."

"No kidding?" It was the ultimate rhetorical question, and ultimately pointless. Had a stray bullet taken his head off, Buck Schotz would have kept on talking.

"Nope. My father worked for the brewery in Milwaukee. Took the name of the beer."

Cody's guess of the name of the beer was Schotz, but a team of Clydesdales couldn't have pulled another word from him.

"And my mom was a hunter. Dropped a seven-pointer on the first morning of deer season, and dropped me that afternoon. Ha, ha. No kidding. "Sort of like the way Indians name their kids, ya know?"

Involuntarily Cody's head twitched a no.

"Yeah, well, seems that when they conceive a kid, ya know, after sex," he paused to make sure the reporter understood the procedure, forcing another involuntary twitch, this one vertical.

"First thing they see, that's what they name him."

Something about the bludgeoning subtlety of his tone signaled that this was a joke, one Cody had actually heard, years earlier – and had repeated because it was funny – but now he was going to hear it again.

"Actually, I overheard a Pawnee chief explaining this to his young son. He said, that's why your sister is named Moon over Woods, and your brother is named Running Bear, and you, my youngest son, are called Two Dogs Fucking."

The laughter that followed was raucous if genuine, with spittle flying in all directions. It was during the racking coughing fit that inevitably followed – Buck consumed fast food, beer, and cigarettes to excess – that Cody wiped the residue from the notebook sitting on his lap, using a Taco Bell napkin he retrieved from the shelf under the rear window of the newscar.

He was amazed, truly amazed, that KMTY was still on the air. He didn't understand why advertisers bought air time, why viewers didn't change channels, why the FCC had failed to yank their license, or why any number of civic organizations hadn't hired an arsonist. And now he was part of the team. He sighed inside, and again was pleased to recognize a feeling that his time on this alien planet was short.

"How'd it go?" Nick Belotti asked when they returned. Cody caught a whiff of something in his question that suggested Belotti was well aware of Schotz's potential...for destruction.

"Oh," Cody managed off-handedly, "I don't think the camera picked up many of his comments."

The look he got back was a smorgasbord of fear, dread, and disgust, with maybe a soupçon of gratitude, for what, Cody might have guessed, but at that point he didn't care. Still, he added, "I don't think anyone will bring charges," before disappearing down the hall to wash his hands of the glamour that was television news.

IX

"But what made you choose the house?"

"You are persistent, Deki-san." To refer to a man this way was a sign of respect.

"You have to know that there are no accidents."

Cody's face showed, cautiously, that he didn't know that. Cody could almost see him sigh. "Synchronicity?" he ventured hopefully. Those hopes were dashed.

Deki didn't make him feel stupid; he did that himself. Well not stupid, really; just totally out of his element. Like he was in a foreign country, or maybe another dimension. Not dangerous, just foreign, and he had to learn the language, and the customs.

"Do you have a god?" he asked gingerly.

The reporter shrugged, "Not in the official sense; you know, old man, long white flowing robes, long white beard." He paused to see if he was on the same track. Deki nodded encouragingly. Cody asked, "Do you?"

"No and yes," his neighbor answered with expected inscrutability. "Like you, I don't have the image of that old man, the father in heaven as the West would have it be." He hunched forward on the sofa, and leaned forward to pour them both more plum wine. "I am Japanese, but my spiritual learning is really from the Lao-Tse, the Tao." He looked at him for recognition, but Cody could offer none. He stood up and went over to the bookshelf and pulled out a small dog-eared paperback book, returned, and handed it to him.

"*The Tao of Pooh*?" he read the title aloud, pronouncing Tao with a "t" sound. As in Winnie the Pooh he gathered from the cover drawing of A.A. Milne's bear flying a kite. He thumbed through the pages quickly. Plenty of drawings, large type. "Are you loaning this to me to read?"

"If you would take the time, I think you will find it most enlightening." He bowed slightly toward the book in his hands. "The Tao," said Deki, pronouncing it with a "d," "is perhaps 4,500 years old. One of many Chinese philosophies, but one of only two to still survive."

"The other being?"

"The other being Confucianism. Come, let us eat." He gestured, and Cody followed him to the dining room table.

Over an excellent meal that was really a sampler of Japanese cuisine – sushi, shumai, gyoza, and tempura – his neighbor described some of the tenets of Taoism, mostly through parables. The bottom line, which it was in the reporter's nature to seek, was that the foundation of the Tao was a healthy relationship between people and nature, water finding it's own level, and taking life the way it is.

Deki took back the book, carefully thumbed a few pages, and almost immediately found a section he wanted. He handed it back to him, pointing to a paragraph that began with Christopher Robin explaining to Pooh about an ancient Chinese painting called "The Vinegar Tasters".

"You can read this while I clear the table."

Normally Cody would have offered to help, but there was something less formal and more comfortable in their quickly budding relationship that allowed him to stay in his chair and pick up the book. In a few paragraphs, the author described the painting.

Confucius, Buddha, and Lao-tse – a "founder" of Taoism – are standing behind a table on which is a pitcher of vinegar. Each is holding a spoon and has tasted the vinegar, which is representative of life. On Confucius' face is a sour expression, illustrating the Confucian belief that life is to be lived rigidly, according to a strict set of rules. Buddha is wearing a bitter expression, representative of the Buddhist philosophy that life with all its pain and hardships is to be endured, until one dies and goes to the better life. And on Lao-tse's face is a smile because vinegar tastes like vinegar, and life is what it is.

Attempting to regain some familiar footing, Cody commented, "Seems reasonable, although some might say this is a little simplistic."

"Simple, yes." The distinction was not lost on Cody. Deki seemed to changed direction. "Why is it that you have no religion? So many from the West go to churches."

"Yes, well, I come from a very enlightened family. My grandparents didn't really believe in a god, and my parents didn't. I was sort of raised with the philosophy that you live, you work hard, you die, and you moulder in the grave." He punctuated the line with hybrid smile and grimace.

Deki was receptive.

Cody continued. "Sounds short-hand, I know. My mother sort of referred to our approach as a bit Calvinist, which was a New England form of Protestantism. I used to call it the Protestant Worth Ethic."

Deki settled back onto his heels. He had known all along why Cody couldn't answer his question about landing in the house next door, but he had used it to open new paths for the journalist to explore. When it came time for Cody to arrive at the real answer, he would have made some interesting discoveries that would create an important foundation for new understanding.

Deki was pleased with the progress his neighbor was making. He had known the enormity of his role in Cody's life, and the concomitant role – as yet undefined – that the younger man would have in his own.

The evening was to be a short one. More plum wine, a dish of green tea ice cream, and before long Cody was ready to go off to his own house, his new old book in hand.

"It was a great meal, Roy." The use of his first name seemed somehow out of place. He corrected with "Deki-san" and continued. "The food was great, and I really enjoyed what we talked about." He surprised himself with the warmth in his voice. He was also vaguely aware that the feeling rose from a deeper place in himself than he had known to exist. It was a genuine and vibrant source.

Deki bowed slightly, and with a look that put the banality of his new friend's words in perspective – while still respecting his tone – he said, "Cody-san, you have much to learn, and much to enjoy."

As he walked down to the street and then up his own driveway, Cody smiled to himself. This was his first day of school, he thought. If Toledo and Monterey were different cultures, the gap between Deki's world and his own was as large. From the impeccable neatness and delicacy of the oriental setting, he thought as he stood in the doorway, surveying the disarray in his living room, to this undefined chaos of his own.

Before going next door to dinner, Cody had arranged most of the furniture, leaving himself to confront stacks of cartons when he got home. He hadn't moved in four years, when he had relocated to Toledo, and that had been something of a hurried affair. Now as he pawed through knick-knacks and assorted miscellany that he had boxed during his years with the network, some important memories were stirred.

He couldn't imagine a world further away, in so many ways, from where he was at that moment. When he would look back in twenty years, when he was sixty, he wondered what his perspective would be on his move to Monterey. He gave himself a gentle, bemused slap on the face. Such speculation was meaningless in the rapidly-changing reality of his new world. His career was heading for a major shift, he had no real ties to anything, and he was learning about the Tao. He laughed aloud. "Good for you," he said to himself.

He piled the boxes of memorabilia, mostly unopened, in a corner of the living room. These would be headed to a storage unit he would rent when he finished the unpacking some time in the next week. Instead he unpacked the rest of his living needs – kitchen and bath stuff and books – into cupboards, drawers and shelves. Hours passed without being counted. When he looked up at the gaudily-painted wooden rooster with a clock on its back that he had been unable to resist on a trip many years ago to Cabo San Lucas, he blanched at the 4:05 it read.

"Don't panic, Cody," he said softly aloud, "the cock's still back on Toledo time." Even though it was three hours earlier, and with most of his unpacking done, he decided to head up to bed. He turned up a corner of his mouth at a small mountain of boxes he had forgotten behind the bedroom door, consigning their unpacking to another day. A cursory scrub of the face – pausing briefly to look for something in the eyes; just curiosity – and he was in bed and headed for dreams.

X

"Didn't you work with Francie LeVillard? In New York?" Beth's call had woken him, and after the usual "oh, sorry" and "doesn't matter" she had gotten to the reason for her early call. Not early for her, of course, it being a minute after eleven in Connecticut, but early for him at a minute after eight in California.

It was Saturday morning. He had awakened two hours earlier, seen the enveloping fog through his bedroom window, smiled, and gone back to sleep. He'd been up late again, unpacking boxes, moving things around in the kitchen, and listening to Sixties music on Pandora as he did so. He loved the music from that decade, even though he hadn't even been born yet. Actually, he loved the whole Sixties decade for the amazing history that it wrote. But while the facts stimulated his mind, the music spoke to his soul.

At one point, closing in on midnight, he'd gone outside to make sure that it wasn't too loud – it wasn't – and he saw a light on in his neighbor's house. It had given him pause, enough so that he stood for a long moment, simply looking in the direction his friend's house. With soft eyes, he noted to himself with a smile.

Deki-san had used the term the night before when he had stopped by Cody's house in the early evening to drop off some hand-rolled sushi made with fresh crab and cilantro. He had a friend, he told the reporter, who was a fisherman who cast his lines with soft eyes. "It is when you see without looking." And then to clear up the confusion that was apparent on the reporter's face, the man explained the meaning of soft eyes.

"First you must know the expression yes, that a picture is worth..." and he let it trail off.

"A thousand words," Cody replied automatically.

Deki smiled. He looked past the reporter into his living room, and at the bookshelves that lined one wall. "Ah, yes, you have a Bartlett's."

Cody was startled that he had spotted the book, and immediately, amidst the hundreds that crowded the floor-to-ceiling bookcases. Deki smiled as he read the response and continued to look into the new friend's face until Cody nodded and went to retrieve the book. He opened it as he returned and quickly found the reference.

"An ancient Chinese saying: 'A picture is worth ten thousand words.' Oh my goodness, I always thought it was a thousand."

"So interesting, yes? But also so true." Deki bowed his head in respect to the revelation. "Another truth, a metaphor of fact from modern science, is that you only see three-thousandths of what your eyes actually perceive."

Cody cocked his head. If he had been at all put out that his neighbor had interrupted his unpacking, the annoyance had disappeared in a flash. And now his mind churned with pleasure over his new learning. "And the rest of what we perceive, we do that with soft eyes. We see it but we don't register it?"

"Very good," Deki said, with a smile and another slight bow of his head. "And when you look at the world with soft eyes, you see much more. Often it is more important than what you were looking at."

Cody chuckled. "No doubt."

"You should eat," he said, nodding toward the plate he'd put on dining room table, "while you are doing your work here," he said. "It is good to nourish the body and the soul together." He bowed again slightly, and said "Good night," and was gone.

"Thank you," Cody said to the disappearing figure. He stood looking out into the fading light and then closed the door. Over the next couple of hours, he nibbled and sorted his way through his belongings. When he'd finished the sushi, he noticed how good he was feeling. Not only had his earlier hunger gone, but he was enjoying a sense of well-being. "Magic Japanese herbs," he said aloud and laughed.

He had been surprised to hear Beth's voice, and surprised that her calling him hadn't evoked more pleasure. In fact, he noted, it felt like something of an intrusion and that was new to him. Was it because his sense of home was different? He let the question go and answered Beth's.

"Washington. She was at the NBC affiliate when I was at State."

"That was what, ten years ago?"

"That's right, about. Why?"

"She's in your neck of the woods. The Monterey Peninsula. She's a detective."

"No kidding," Cody said, more than interested with the news. "A detective," he repeated.

"A consulting detective," Beth said. "According to what I read."

"What was it you were reading?"

There was hesitation at the other end of the line, enough to inform him. "Oh," he said, which meant he understood. Beth's father was retired CIA. Probably CIA. She'd never been explicit, for obvious reasons. And despite the considerable value she, using information from her father, might have been to Cody, she had never even come close to crossing the line of her father's confidence in her. It wasn't just propriety; it was security. And not just national but personal. People in his line of business showed professional courtesy not to involve relatives, as long as those relatives didn't become actors in their insular play.

"She's playing with the big boys." It wasn't a question and he didn't get an answer. "I'll look her up."

The rest of the call was little more than perfunctory; howyadoin' and the weather. When Cody got off the phone, if it might have sounded quickly to Beth, it was because he was feeling excitement at the prospect of hooking up with Francie LeVillard again. It might have mollified Beth if he had told her why; that his feelings about Francie were professional. She had been one of the most serious journalists in local news in the nation's capital, and journalism had been missing from his life for all too long.

He googled her and found very few local references. He thought of calling Channel 13 but he didn't know the people who worked on weekends. He might have called Felice Inez at home, but decided that would be an intrusion, perhaps not unwanted, that he didn't need to inflict on her. He could wait until Monday to track down Francie LeVillard.

XI

It had been a while since Cody had looked forward to a Monday morning, and this occasion wasn't about work anyway. According to one of the very few news bits that Google had turned up about Francie LeVillard, she had worked closely with Monterey County Sheriff Telford "Bogie" Spivac. Cody Howard called Spivac's office, informing his executive assistant that he was a new reporter in town, and wanted to introduce himself. It wasn't long before the Sheriff himself called back.

"I used to see you reporting from Afghanistan. You were good," the sheriff said. "Then I didn't see you. What, four years ago or something?"

Cody was surprised that someone remembered his work, let alone appreciated it. "Thanks, Sheriff. I didn't know anyone would have remembered me from those days."

"A friend of mine is another serious journalist. She said you had come to town. She said she had known you back then when she was a reporter in Washington. Francie LeVillard."

Cody laughed. "Small world, Sheriff. In truth, that was why I was calling you. I heard from a friend back east over the weekend that she was here and I wanted to see her again."

The sheriff gave Cody his email address and told him to send him a note and he would reply with Francie's contact information. "And let's get together for a beer or something. I'd like to hear what you've been doing and what brought you to the Central Coast."

"I'd like that, Sheriff."

"And talk about what happened at Soledad last week."

Cody took a moment to take that in; a noticeable moment.

"This is a small community," the sheriff told him.

"I guess," Cody replied. "When would you like that beer?"

"I'll check my calender and let you know."

Cody sent out an email from his personal account, rather than the station's, in part because he didn't know if Burgess accessed his employees e-traffic, and also because he sensed that it was less likely that he would be at the station very long. A minute later, he got a reply from the sheriff with Francie's info. "As it happens, I'm free this evening if you are. We could grab a bite at Fandangos. Seven o'clock, if that works for you."

"Great, see you there at seven," Cody wrote back. He felt a surge of energy that raised a smile on his face. He hadn't experienced such a spike since his early days at the network. He felt alive again, which was both exhilarating and thought-provoking.

Why had he fallen so far? What had invigorated him? What could he do to maintain this feeling? As these questions passed through his mind, they also generated images. Including those of Francie LeVillard from way back when and of Deki-san of that weekend.

"Howard!" came the shout from the assistant news director. Cody walked over to Belotti's desk, realizing that the dread he had experienced the previous week was gone. It was, he thought, like the feeling a person has when he's given two weeks notice. Suddenly most of what had been bothering him was gone. Still, not knowing what was next, he kept his true thoughts under wraps.

"Yes, sir," he said to Belotti. He had tried to keep his voice neutral as before, but even Belotti had heard a difference, though he lacked the depth to know what he was hearing.

"Yeah, you're going out on your own. Strut your stuff." The sneer was back but without much energy behind it. Belotti knew he was wholly out-matched.

"Whatcha got?" Cody proffered genially, engendering a flicker of cautious suspicion in the man.

"Yeah, I want you to go over to the P.G. golf course restaurant. There's a guy who lives across the street who's been trying to shut it down for years. He says the place makes too much noise. They want to stay open until ten instead of seven. The city council is thinking about it. Here," he said, handing the reporter a newspaper clipping. "It's all in here."

"What kind of coverage do you want? A full report for the early and voice-over for the late?"

"Yeah," Belotti said, apparently surprised that Cody had picked up anything during the previous week when he'd gone out with the other reporters. "You've got Inez. She's on another shoot. She'll meet you there in 20 minutes."

"Right," Cody said, turned on his heel and headed for his debut assignment. He drove across Monterey to the western tip of The Peninsula where the Pacific Ocean meets Monterey Bay, providing glorious views for the golfers playing the links. It wasn't by any measure like the pro-designed courses at nearby Pebble Beach, but it offered a delightful venue for duffers who just liked to play the municipal course, and for just a tenth of what the high-priced spreads charged.

Across the street from the pro shop on the edge of the course was The Grille, an unassuming but surprisingly bright restaurant that served the golfers, early to late, as well as local groups like Rotary and the DAR. Edna Stacey was renewing her lease with the city, and was asking an extension of her hours so she could serve dinners and finally break even after seven years.

"The community is all in favor," Ms. Stacey said to Cody as Felice Inez's camera rolled. "The people who live in the area would love to walk over here for dinner. And the Planning Commission said it would enhance the night life in P.G. in addition to putting five figures more in the city pot. The only objection has come for the man who lives over there," she pointed across the parking lot, some public tennis courts, and a green belt. "He says it would make too much noise. Bah! We're not having a bunch of loud drunks. These are good folks who come to enjoy a nice dinner."

As Cody noted in his stand-up close, "The Grille has been open on a trial basis for six months, and a survey of its neighbors fielded only one complaint."

That complaint came from Elmont Hedges who told the Channel 13 viewers that he had a right to block the permanent extension of hours because he'd lived in his house for more than thirty years, and that gave him rights. He wasn't explicit about what rights he had, but he was adamant. He said he had money, and he'd spend his last dime on lawyers to block The Grille and elect new council members if the current members voted for The Grille.

During his interview with the avowed obstacle, Cody asked, "Mr. Hedges, why should you alone be allowed to block this business from providing a dining opportunity that locals can walk to, hiring four new people, and generating $60,000 for the city?"

Hedges, a basset hound-mournful looking man of 75, peered at the reporter for a good thirty seconds before he spoke. "You're on their side. You're not supposed to take sides." Then he started cussing out Cody like a sailor.

When it appeared that the man wasn't going to stop, Cody cut it. "Stop that! Who do you think you are speaking to another human being that way? I asked you a reasonable question, one to which the community has a right to an answer. I'll give you another chance to answer it, but please, sir, don't be indecent to them or to me."

The old man looked shell-shocked. He stood mute for fifteen seconds and then slowly shuffled away. Cody later heard that no one had ever stood up to him, and he didn't know how to be called on his behavior. Of course, being the professional that he was, Cody kept that confrontation with Hedges out of his report, but that didn't stop someone at the station from posting it on *YouTube* after the early news had run.

The first comments, some of them in very ugly terms, charged Cody with self-promotion and with beating up on an old man. There were a couple of phone calls to Channel 13 threatening to kill Cody and promising to burn down the station, but the tide quickly turned with a number of people, particularly from the business community, praising Cody for standing up to cantankerous bully.

When Cody arrived at Fandangos, an hour-plus after the early newscast had finished, the sheriff, upon meeting him for the first time, joked, "You sure came out of the box in a hurry."

Cody raised his eyebrows. "You watched the news?"

"Not usually, but because we were meeting tonight. Plus I saw the *YouTube* video."

Cody shook his head. "You know that wasn't me who posted it. I don't know who did it. Most unfortunate."

"Oh I don't think so. It's what people have wanted to say to that putz for a long time."

The reporter laughed, "I haven't heard that word since I was on the east coast."

Moments later the headwaiter came up to their table to welcome the sheriff, and when he was introduced to Cody, he said, "You were on *YouTube*! My wife sent me the link. Thank you. Even though they will be our competitor, they are good people there, and not too close."

Cody nodded his appreciation.

"So what would you like to drink? The first round is on the house."

Cody began to protest but the sheriff waved him off. "This is a small town. A drink is not a bribe, it's just a way of saying 'welcome.'"

"Well, thank you," he told the headwaiter, and ordered a glass of Scheid Pinot. The sheriff asked for his usual, which when delivered two minutes later turned out to be a Sierra Nevada pale ale.

The sheriff raised his glass to the reporter. "Welcome to The Peninsula," he said and they clinked glasses. "I hope as many people watch your news as apparently saw the video."

Cody laughed.

"So you may have guessed that I'm a news junkie. I saw you reporting from Afghanistan and before that, you were doing weekends at the State Department, right?"

Cody nodded.

"I read up on you about leaving the network and going to work with the U.N. peacekeepers and then getting thrown out. You were lucky. But then Toledo, and now Monterey? You're too good for this market."

Cody smiled at the sheriff. "I think that's the nicest thing anyone has ever said about my work." He sipped the wine and thought for a moment. "I should have given this some thought myself. I guess I've been on auto-pilot for the last five years. Yes, I know the news, and journalism has been a calling for me. But the networks aren't relevant any more, and the local stations are mostly about personalities. They haven't been about news for years. Stations like this one will stop doing news when they no longer at least break even. That time is coming soon."

"As their audience dies off."

"Yes. The younger audience, the under-sixty crowd, isn't reading newspapers or watching television news. Why should they? By the time the news comes on, or the paper is delivered, the news is old. The stories have changed."

"So what does that mean for you?"

Cody chuckled. "Dunno. I have nine months on my contract with Enlaw. If I last that long. I suppose I need to think about my future."

"Teach?"

Cody shrugged. "Possibly, although I'd be haunted by the phrase, 'People who can, do. People who can't, teach.'"

The two men laughed. The waiter came over with his order book in hand. "Manuel," said the sheriff, "I don't think we're quite ready to order yet, but why don't you bring us some of your world-famous clam chowder. I'm sure my friend from the east coast would like to try it." Then the sheriff's eyes shifted toward the entrance. "Make that three bowls." Then he stood up. Cody turned in that direction and a broad grin opened on his face.

The two men rose to their feet as Francie LeVillard approached the table. An attractive brunette wearing a navy suede blazer over a beige blouse and dark pants. "Hi, honey," said the sheriff as she leaned over and gave him a hug. Then she turned to Cody and looked him up and down. She might have just taken his hand, but her warm smile belied her pleasure at seeing him. She leaned forward and embraced him.

"So good to see you, Cody. A fellow refugee from what was once the news."

"Good to see you, too, Francie. You look great. There is life after news."

The three laughed and Francie sat down in the chair the sheriff held out for her next to him.

The headwaiter arrived immediately. "Good evening, Miss Francie. So nice to see you again."

"Thank you, Manuel."

"A glass of the Bernardus Chardonnay this evening?"

"Perfect," she replied. Then she turned to Cody, furrowing her brow in thought. "I was trying to remember the last time I saw you. I think it was at State before you went back to Afghanistan."

"Six years maybe," Cody suggested.

"My goodness, we were both still young then." They laughed. "I was so surprised to hear from Bogie that you were at KMTY, and not as news director but as a reporter. Are you being punished?" There was more laughter.

Cody gave them the short version of his downward spiral, provoking the slow empathetic shaking of two heads. He finished by reprising the sheriff's question about his future and his response.

"Well, Cody, I have to tell you, from personal experience, that this is a great place to figure out what you want to do. I had no plans when I got here."

"And she is now the world's finest consulting detective since the great Sherlock Holmes," the sheriff said with a strong note of pride in his voice. "And I'm not exaggerating. I've never seen anyone like her."

"Oh, pshaw, Bogie," Francie said, nudging him with her shoulder. "It's just a hobby."

"Hobby, schmobby, my esteemed colleague. You've busted some major cases that the feds hadn't even been aware of." He told Cody, "She discovered terrorists smuggling nuclear triggers into this country. And she stopped the Russian mob from assassinating a double agent. Don't get on her bad side."

There was more laughter. The waiter arrived with the clam chowder and the menus. The three started in on the chowder. "Mmm, this is good," Cody reviewed appreciatively. "Almost as good as the best I ever had, at the Land Ho in Orleans on Cape Cod. I almost missed a flight it was so good." And then he added, "but this is at least a close second."

"You'll have to try the sand dabs, Cody," the sheriff told him. "They don't have sand dabs on the east coast, I don't think."

And that's what he ordered for his entree. Then he began to question them about the market and the station. He talked about his new home and he promised to invite them both for dinner when everything was unpacked, He added that he thought he might invite his fascinating neighbor, Roy Deki, to join them. He saw them exchange knowing glances at the mention of his name. "So you know, Deki-san?"

The two looked again at each other and tacitly it was up to the sheriff to tell the story. "First off, you're lucky to have such a fine man next door. Not that you would ever need him, but if you did, he'd be there for you without asking. He showed up on my radar when he had a restaurant on Sixty-Eight. It was a small place serving traditional Japanese food. He didn't do any advertising, but word of mouth quickly made it very successful. He opened a second place on The Wharf," he winced, "and that's when he ran into problems.

"There was a gang of young toughs who were running a protection racket. It was a half-dozen small-time crooks, not demanding much, but ugly. They told Roy that he had to pay them. He refused. They painted slurs on the face of his place but Roy simply repainted the place the next morning and was open for lunch that same day.

"A couple of weeks later, two of the gang attacked him in the parking lot when he was leaving for the night. They had knives and were going to cut him up, but he's a black belt in *aikido*. He took their knives away from them, broke one of the guy's arms and dislocated the jaw on the other. They ran off, and Roy drove up to the police station and filed a report. A week later, the gang got a shyster lawyer to file assault charges against him."

"Two against one?" Cody guessed.

The sheriff nodded. "Roy got a very good lawyer who advised him to hire Francie to do some digging. Which she did." He looked over at her and she shook her head. He continued, "Our friend here found out that one of The Wharf owners was actually behind the gang. She got enough evidence to take to the U.S. attorney in San Francisco who indicated the owner and the gang members on RICO charges."

"But not a happy ending?" Cody asked, looking at the glum faces.

Francie recounted, "There's a lot of family connections in Monterey, Cody, and someone, we were pretty sure that we knew who but there wasn't any proof, who was associated with one of the gang members, took it upon himself to strike back at Deki. He put arsenic in some of his food. Not enough to kill anyone, but a lot of people got sick. Deki closed his restaurants the next day."

"Jeez. And they never got the person who did this. That seems like a big crime not to go unsolved."

The two exchanged glances again. "Off the record?" the sheriff asked.

Cody nodded. "Sure."

Francie finished the story. "It was the sister of the restaurant owner behind the gang. A nasty piece of work. The family sent her home, back to the old country. Lebanon?" she asked the sheriff.

"Or Jordan. Somewhere over there."

"When was that?" Cody asked.

"About four years ago," the sheriff answered.

"And he didn't re-open?"

Francie shook her head.

"I spoke with him privately. He told me he didn't have faith in the

Monterey police, and he said there were probably too many of the gang for him to kill without someone finding, or planting, evidence on him."

"Seriously, he said that?" Cody had trouble imaging the man he met even thinking about such a thing, letting alone admitting such thoughts to the sheriff.

"Oh yes, and he was quite matter-of-fact about it."

"Deki-san is a very true man. He believes in justice as if it were a religion. I've trained with him on the *aikido* mat," Francie said. "He's incredibly present. His mind doesn't wander. He's all about order in the universe."

"Amazing," Cody said, "I've had a couple of conversations with him and it feels to me like he fills the room. Not intrusively, more like all knowing, if that makes sense."

Francie smiled at him. "Yes, that's Deki-san. I don't think you need to let him know that you know what happened, though I'm sure he will expect that you will learn about it. In any event, Cody, know that you are blessed to have him as your neighbor."

The dinner stretched past closing but they were only hurried out eventually by their own next day's schedule. New friendships were made, and Cody learned more about the area that he now called home. Francie and the sheriff took turns explaining how the county was split by the tourist-centric Peninsula and the agriculture-dominated Salinas Valley, and how they were culturally divided by "the lettuce wall."

They also confirmed what he had already learned about Soledad: the corruption of the administrators and guards, and the prison being run by the inmates. Cody wanted to know why something wasn't done about it.

"Because until we legalize drugs in this country," the sheriff said, "it produces too much profit which has bought control of the system. Everyone's paid off. Even if just marijuana was decriminalized, it would pull enough money out of the system so the gangs couldn't grease the wheels."

"And if we decrim'd cocaine and heroin," Francie put in, "we could restore justice across the country. The cops could focus on real crime, the courts wouldn't be clogged, and the prisons could be used to lock away all the violent people."

Cody shook his head. "If only we had some leadership in this country."

XII

When Cody arrived at the station the next morning, he learned that Herb Burgess had ordered Nick Belotti to instruct their new reporter not to make waves. But not five minutes later, Big Don appeared in the news room and announced to all assembled, which comprised Cody, Belotti, and Lane Headworthy, that while he didn't countenance someone posting the piece on *YouTube*, he was very pleased with the general outpouring of support from the community.

Cody could sense a new feeling in the news room, but he was far too practical to think anyone was going to get excited about real journalism. His cautious pessimism was ratified when his assignment that morning was to attend a meeting of the Monterey County Water Allocation Agency where there would be a discussion of measures to deal with the drought. Actually, it got interesting.

Keith Myers, the agency director, outlined the arid numbers dealing with the lack of rainfall, and one of his staffers talked about programs to induce homeowners and businesses to cut down on water usage. It was not news. Hotels needed to wash linens less often. Restaurants needed to stop serving water unless it was requested. Residents needed to use water-consuming appliances less often, and reduce watering in the yards.

Fergy had shot the event and was about to pack up when Cody told him he wanted to do an interview. He walked them through the office warren to find Myers alone in his office.

"I'm Cody Howard. Can I ask you a couple of questions for Channel 13?"

Myers gave him a big grin. "Well okay, if you promise not to beat me up like you did that guy in Pacific Grove."

They both laughed and then he asked, "Have you eaten at The Grille?"

Cody shook his head.

"Nice spot. Good food, too. You want to try it."

"Thanks, I will." Cody saw that his cameraman was perched against the back wall, his camera pointing over the reporter's shoulder, ready to shoot. Cody gave him a nod and began.

"These anti-drought measures that were discussed today, they seem logical. What I don't understand, and it's probably because I'm new to the area, but why weren't these measures enacted two years ago when the drought started? For that matter, why aren't they always in effect, except when there's been a lot of rain for a long time?"

Myers gave him a thoughtful look. Then he looked at the ceiling before he returned his eyes to the reporter. "Those are very fair questions. The simple answer is politics. There is constant political pressure on the elected officials by the business interests in the area to let them have all the water they want, without any restrictions. On The Peninsula, the hospitality industry wants to wash everything every day when no one I know washes their sheets and towels but maybe once a week...if that.

"Now I appreciate it's nice to have clean fresh sheets on the bed but people staying at the hotels and motels for three days certainly won't go somewhere else because they're sleeping on the same sheets.

"And with the restaurants, the truth is that if they only served water when people asked for it instead of automatically, and only refilled glasses when requested, we'd save enough water to avoid the need for the drastic cutbacks that will be headed our way soon enough."

"You're saying that the politicians haven't stood up to the business interests?"

"I'm saying they might have gotten out in front on this issue and we wouldn't be in as bad a situation as we are today."

"Let me guess, they're not going to be happy you saying this publically."

Myers sighed. "I should have been banging this drum two years ago. They heard from me then, but they didn't act. If they don't want to hear the truth, they should find someone else to be their front man."

"Again, I'm new to the area, but could the agriculture industry be doing a better job conserving water?"

"You are after my job, aren't you?" Myers said with a laugh. He sighed deeply. "Again, the simple answer is 'yes, of course they could.' We have had private meetings with the ag people, offering ideas for how they could let The Peninsula have more of their water without in any way cutting into their operations. They have been, how shall I say this, reticent."

"But why, this is all Monterey County? If they have water they don't need and The Peninsula is drying up, why won't they help?"

"Because there has long been a feud between ag and The Peninsula. Have you heard the term 'the lettuce wall'?"

"Yes, just last night."

"It exists in a big way. It's both financial and cultural. It's a natural conflict between the farmers with mud on their boots and the spit-shine hospitality folks pocketing two billion a year for producing obsequious smiles. Monterey has the restaurants with the beautiful water views. Salinas has the gangs. There's a lot of resentment, in both directions, and the ag people control the water."

Cody sat still for a long moment. Then he turned back to his cameraman and told him he was done, that he would meet him in the car. When he had left, Cody asked the water manager, "Is this going to put your job in jeopardy? I mean, I don't know the players but I've been around enough to know that politicians are truth-averse, especially when someone is telling the truth about their failures."

Myers eyed the reporter. "Maybe you came at the right time. You tracked me down to my office. You asked the right questions. I have to tell you, I've been waiting for two years for someone to ask me what you just did. Would I have told them what I've just told you? I don't know. Maybe if I was having a bad day. And maybe it is time for me to leave. But I work for the people of this county, not the politicians. If it's time for me to go, fine. I've had more offers for more satisfying jobs paying twice what I'm making here than I could shake a stick at."

"So why have you stayed?"

"I thought maybe I could make a difference."

"A lot of 'maybes'."

"Hope springs eternal."

Cody got up and extended his hand to Myers who shook it firmly. "You know, I would kill this interview if you asked?"

"Yes, I appreciate that, but go ahead and run it."

"What we just talked about now, after the camera guy left, that's just between us."

Myers laughed. "What are you doing in this business? I've dealt with the press for 18 years and I can't remember ever talking to someone with your integrity. Especially in this market."

"I guess I take my work as seriously as you take yours."

"Good for you."

Cody turned to leave. Myers stopped him. "Hey, how about I take you to The Grille, show you what a fine place you may have helped to save?"

"I'd like that."

Myers took a business card from the holder on his desk and wrote something on the back of it before handing it to the reporter. My private cell. Give me a call and we'll set a date."

Cody left the building and got into the car. "What did you think?" he asked the cameraman who ostensibly couldn't speak English but just shot where the reporter pointed.

The man looked long and hard at the reporter. "I think you got a really big story."

"We did," Cody agreed. "I just worry that they might not run it."

Fergy raised his eyebrows. He hadn't thought about it, but he suddenly knew it was a possibility. "So maybe I should make a copy of it for you, before they see it?"

"Yeah, I think that would be a good idea. I hope I don't have to use it, but news is news even if the big bosses don't like it."

XIII

"We got some good stuff from Keith Myers," Cody told Belotti when he walked into the newsroom.

"Oh yeah," the producer responded without looking up. "Myers never has anything to say."

"He did today," Cody affirmed, fingering the flash drive with the back-up of the interview in his pocket. "It's probably the lead."

Belotti looked up at him with an annoyed expression. "Howard, I'll decide what goes where in my newscast, all right? I don't need some network reject telling me what to use and how."

"Actually, Belotti," said the reporter with a genuine smile, "you do need someone telling you because you lack even the most basic news judgement. And if you don't pull your head out of your ass, I'll take this upstairs. And maybe we'll be trading desks."

Cody turned away and went back to the editing room where Fergy had cued up the morning shoot. He picked out the sound cuts that he would use, noted the in-cues, out-cues, and running times, and returned to his desk to write his script. It didn't take him fifteen minutes. He brought a copy to Fergy who looked it over and nodded. Then he brought another copy to Belotti.

"Here ya go. Fergy can shoot my on-camera pieces at my desk, if that's all right with you."

Belotti stared at the reporter for a long moment and then read the script. His eyebrows rose. When he finished, he looked back up at Cody. "You really got this stuff. And it's exclusive."

"I knew you'd like it."

"It's dynamite, but hey, I gotta get upstairs to sign off on it." He got up hurriedly from his desk and headed for the exit. Cody smiled and returned to his desk. It was ten minutes before Belotti came back, stopping by the reporter's desk. Burgess ran it past Big Don who said to go with it.

"Gonna lead with it, Nick?" he asked.

"Yeah," the producer said, and then quietly added, "Of course."

Fergy returned from the editing room with his camera and set up to shoot Cody at his desk. In two minutes he'd recorded the short on-camera pieces and the voice-overs. He went back to the edit room to assemble the spot.

It wasn't much later that Belotti called, "Hey, um, Cody..."

The reporter got up from his desk and stood at the opening of his cubicle. "Yessir," he replied.

"How 'bout you and Fergy head over to Carmel this afternoon. There's gonna be a march from the downtown park to city hall to protest against the city administrator."

"In quaint and proper Carmel?"

"Uh-huh. There's copy in today's paper and I'll email you the press release from the woman who's organizing it. Starts at 3:30."

"Right. Do you want a full report, or just some voice-over and sound cuts?"

"Probably just v-o, maybe a coupla talking heads if they're any good."

"Okay, and I'll call in if we get anything exciting. Otherwise back here in time to cut some voice-over and sound."

The march attracted about a hundred people, mostly locals enjoying the lovely weather and the opportunity to socialize. The march organizer was pleased and happily said so on camera. The city administer had nothing to say, but the mayor said from the steps of city hall that the city council had full confidence in their administrator. Cody called in to tell Belotti what he had and wrote a quick voice-over script for one of the anchors, leading into two short sound cuts. He went over it with Fergy who would take care of the editing. When they got back to the office, Cody typed up the voice-over script and production cues and handed them in.

Then he looked again at the note that had been left on his desk. It was from Herb Burgess. It said, "See me. In the morning." Cody toyed briefly with the idea of going up stairs then, but shelved it. He had no idea whether he was going to receive kudos or another hostile shot – it was hard to know what was happening in this station – but decided that it could certainly wait until morning.

He sat at his desk and watched the early evening news. He was pleased to see that there were no major technical errors that evening, and none with his contributions to the show. He slipped out of the office just as Ron and Lara were saying their goodnights and he went home. He wanted to complete the unpacking, break down the empty boxes, and store them in his garage.

On the way home, he stopped at the Trader Joe's and loaded his cart with everything he could imagine he would want to find in his cupboards and refrigerator. Plus he added many goodies to snack on. Cody preferred to nosh over the course of an evening rather than sit down for a meal. When he got to the check-out counter, a friendly clerk looked at the over-loaded cart and asked, "Did you just move here?"

Cody laughed. "Yes, as a matter of fact. From back east. Toledo, to be precise."

"Well welcome to Monterey. I hope you like it here."

"Why thank you," Cody replied. "More and more I think I will."

Indeed he had had a very good day and he looked forward to his evening at home. It was less about what he would find in the cartons that clogged the living room and the second bedroom that would be his office, and more that he was putting down roots. He had known his network "homes" would be temporary, and he certainly had no intention of living in Toledo beyond his contract. But here on the Monterey Peninsula, he had a sense of permanence he'd not felt since childhood.

"Very interesting," he said to himself as he pulled into his driveway. "Not having plans had delivered what I hadn't even thought to want." He wasn't worried about leaving his three-year-old Camry outside, since it had weathered the ice and salt of Toledo for that many winters. He would keep it in the garage once he had sorted out all of his things. He had to make three trips from the car to the kitchen, and when he was done, he stood for a moment thinking of how he wanted to arrange things in the cupboards and the refrigerator. Then he unpacked the food and put it away. Except for some cold cuts to nibble on while he attacked the boxes in the living room. He also moved a bottle of Prosecco brut from the refrigerator to the freezer for 20 minutes. He liked his first taste of bubbly to be very cold.

A few moments later, the chimes at his door rang. Cody frowned at the interruption. He wanted the evening for himself. It was, as he expected, his neighbor, who wasn't going to be an interruption at all.

"My esteemed friend," he said, "I am very aware of your need not to have company, but I thought you might enjoy this book," he said, "handing a CD to Cody. "It's 'The Tao of Pooh' that I gave you, but in audio form. You might enjoy listening to it as you unpack." With that he bowed slightly and began to withdraw.

"Deki-san," Cody said before the man could turn away. "I am very grateful to have found my home next door to you. I know that you are very important to me. Thank you." And with that, he bowed slightly to his neighbor who smiled slightly, turned and left. Cody waited a few moments until Deki-san had walked back to his house and he had heard the front door close.

Four hours later, shortly after midnight, he had finished unpacking most of the cartons, broken down the empties, and stacked them in the garage. He had also listened to the audiobook and finished half the bottle of Prosecco. Part of his unpacking had revealed his champagne bottle stopper, which eliminated his need to use a spoon, the metal shaft having kept the effervescence. Somehow it did, as he knew from experience, but he didn't know how.

"A metaphor, that," he said aloud, as he walked through the living room, turning off the sound system and the lights and heading up to bed.

XIV

When he got into the office the next morning, Cody had forgotten that he was supposed to see Herb Burgess when he got in. But Nick Belotti told him that Burgess was out at a doctor's appointment and it wasn't important anyway. The reporter in him wondered briefly what it might have been that the news director wanted to see him about but then realized it would be a waste of time to even speculate so he forced it from his mind.

Work was not a real challenge that third day though it did present its own opportunity for Cody Howard to push ahead on a story he thought would have some meat on it. He had been sent to the county courthouse in Salinas to cover the arraignment of two men in their late teens on a series of gang-related charges. Felice Inez used her experience and wile to position herself to capture a few seconds of video of the two walking from a police van into the courthouse holding area. A sketch artist, whose costs were shared by the five-media county pool would supply the rest of the visuals.

It was in the hallway outside of the courtroom that Cody ran into Sheriff Spivac. Making sure that no one was in earshot, he asked, "Would it serve your purposes to have a story done about what's going on in Soledad? I know it's not your jurisdiction, but you'd have to deal with the fallout."

The sheriff looked around, too, before answering, "As a matter of fact it would, but here is not the place to talk about it. Why don't you stop by my office when the hearing is over."

Cody nodded. "Will do."

And so, after the charges were read and the attorneys for the two alleged gang-bangers had requested a delay in answering them, Cody walked over to the sheriff's office. He introduced himself to

Mona Bothcart, Bogie's secretary, who gave him a knowing smile and said, "Go on in. He's expecting you."

Before Cody had even settled into his chair across from the sheriff, he was prodded, "Are you aware that you'll be stirring up a rat's nest if you report on what's really going on down there?"

"I don't mind stirring things up," Cody replied, perhaps a little too lightly.

"I know you've been in some dirty places, but be warned that some of the toes you're likely to step on are connected with some very nasty players. They like to hurt people."

The tone of the sheriff's voice, even more than his words, got through to the reporter. "I know you don't have a concealed weapons permit. You might think of getting one. Or not. You're probably not mean enough to shoot someone, even if you could pull a gun in time."

"It doesn't say much for our criminal justice system that you're telling me this, Sheriff."

"Call me Bogie. No, it doesn't, but it says a lot about it. You've heard it right. Some of the top drug lords are in Soledad, and they run their drug operations from inside. They manage it because they've paid off, or scared enough, of the prison staff, They don't just punish people who cross them, they torture them before they kill them. Or they rape their wives or daughters.

"Like those two down at the courthouse today. Nineteen and twenty years old. Rap sheets you'd expect in perps twice their age. But these days, they start young, while they're juvies. They do their time, maybe skip a few incarcerations by scaring witnesses into silence. Then they get out because the prisons are over-crowded and because they're not the worst." Bogie took a breath and let it out. "I know you won't be able to report this, but the biggest problem law enforcement has is that the community won't help us."

"But aren't they the ones being ripped off? And hurt?"

"Yeah, and killed. But the gangs have them intimidated, plus the gangs' families are the ones who make up those communities. The people won't rat out their own brothers and sons."

"How do you handle that?"

"That I can't tell you. Off the record I'll say that if there is a really horrendous crime, we have some levers we can pull. But there's always a catch. Maybe someone who gives us information has to leave and never come back."

"Can anyone fix this situation? The feds? The national guard?"

The sheriff shook his head resignedly. "We could clean it up, but it would be politically disastrous. We'd put a fence up around the entire area, and start sorting out the illegal immigrants and the real criminals. That would reduce the population significantly, disrupt the community so it might get put back together properly, but the growers would go nuts because we would be depriving them of their labor force. Plus it would be a struggle to keep the community clean."

"Even though it would be in their best interests."

The sheriff frowned at him. "With where you've been, with what you've seen, you can't still think that people act for themselves. Look at Ferguson where the community gets upset about a single black kid getting shot by a white cop, and without knowing how it really came down, they start a week of looting. What's looting got to do with civil rights or community? They destroyed their own business community. Or look at Gaza, where all those Palestinians let Hamas shoot missiles into Israel, knowing how Israel is going to react.

"This is no different here, except maybe in scope. Poverty, ignorance, violence. A tragedy that cops and courts can't do much about except keep score."

Cody looked hard at the sheriff. "So why are you still sheriff? You're in your third term. You have a great pension. You have a family. You could get a great job in security at a think tank anywhere you want."

"You did some research," he said with a smile that slowly faded and then he explained. "You hear about people saying that they don't like what the United States has become and they're talking about leaving, for Canada or Uruguay or Fiji?"

Cody nodded. "More and more."

"How come you aren't going with them?"

Cody sat up in his chair. "Because I'm an American and I owe it to my country to stay and fix what's wrong. Maybe I can't do anything at the moment, but I'm not going to desert."

The sheriff smiled back him. "Exactly," he said quietly. "This is where I live. My parents came here from Sacramento. I was born here. I'm going to do what I can to make it like it was when my folks moved here. Yeah, I'm like you. I don't know how or when I can fix what's broken, but I'll be here when the time comes. I won't have to move back from anywhere."

He sat quiet for some time, hearing what he had just said. Then he spoke again. "You are new here, but from what little I know about you, and what Francie has said about you, you could be one of the good guys who decides to stay and set his roots here. I just want to make sure that you know what you're getting into, digging in dark corners of our community. Like Soledad."

The reporter reflected for a moment. "Sheriff...Bogie, I appreciate what you are telling me. And I sure take the warning seriously. I've seen some of those bad folks who would just as soon kill me as talk to me. I saw it in New York when I started looking into corruption in Brooklyn and talked with some people from the Russian mob. They were shackled and behind a solid plexiglass barrier, with guards around them, and I couldn't wait to get away from them.

"I saw it in Afghanistan. It was different there. There was a vacant look in the eyes of some of the Taliban. It wasn't like they hated me. It was that I didn't exist to them. It was why the Brits, the Soviets, and the U.S. would never accomplish anything there. We were fighting people who didn't share the basic value of a human life."

The sheriff shook his head in agreement.

"Bogie, why haven't you tried to feed this story out to the press before? Why are you willing to give it to me?"

"Because, Cody, there weren't any reporters in the market I would trust to get the story right; not until you arrived. And Francie vouched for you."

"I walked into it, did I?" the reporter asked and laughed.

"It's not too late to back out," the sheriff said softly. "No one would hold it against you."

"Yeah, I know. Let's see how it goes." He shifted in his chair. "Maybe I shouldn't be asking you this, at least not in your office, but I was a pretty good shot when I was younger. My uncle taught me. We did some hunting, but mostly it was target shooting. Then he took me through a police course in Dallas where they pull up targets right in front of you. Not just targets but also people who you shouldn't shoot."

"I went there a few years ago. How'd you do?"

"I scored in the top ten percent," he said with a smile. "Then I went back about ten years ago. They had a whole different set of images, and they showed with less warning."

"And?"

"I missed one out of twenty."

The sheriff whistled. "That's impressive." He looked hard at the reporter. "What do you suppose made you so good at it? You hadn't been to Afghanistan by then?"

Looking down, remembering, Cody shook his head. He looked back up at the sheriff. "I was ten. My grandparents had a convenience store in Mahwah, New Jersey. I used to sit with my grandpa and he would tell me stories between customers coming in. One day a guy came in with a gun and told my grandpa to give him what was in the register. My grandpa said, okay, that he could have all the money. He opened the register and took out the bills. He asked the robber if he should put the money in a bag for him. The robber was nervous. He nodded his head yes. My grandpa reached for a bag under the counter. The robber later told the cops he thought he was going for a gun because he shot my grandpa in the head and then ran out without the money."

He swallowed hard. "I was brought in to ID him. Ten years old. I loved my grandpa. I wanted to kill the man." He looked at the sheriff. "I guess I still do."

Bogie nodded. "I can see that. You'd be all right to carry a gun. But we have a problem in this state. They passed a law that if you get a carry permit, your name goes on a public list, available online."

"That's nuts," Cody responded.

"Yeah it is." He left it there for a moment. "You didn't hear it from me, but someone said to me recently that if he decided he needed to be armed, it would be without a permit. As the old saying goes, I'd rather be judged by twelve than carried by six."

Cody understood.

"Talk to Francie," the sheriff said.

And that was it for the personal advice. For the next twenty minutes, the sheriff provided the reporter with considerable detail about the Soledad prison, how it was run, locally and from Sacramento, the gangs inside and what they controlled outside. He made it clear what was on and off the record. Then his phone buzzed. It was his secretary reminding him that he had to leave for another appointment.

"That should get you started," he told the reporter. "Call if you have any questions. Oh, and talk to Francie."

Cody thanked the sheriff, for the information and the advice, and headed back to Monterey.

XV

"Got anything hot today?"

Cody shook his head. "Nothing big, Nick. I thought I might get something more, and I did, but nothing to write home about."

The news producer grunted his acknowledgment. The reporter went to his cubicle and wrote up his script.

The sheriff was well aware of how important it was to build up Cody Howard's reputation in the market, and providing him with exclusive information would get him noticed fast. The "nothing big" was some of the evidence against the gangbangers that had been given to the DA but which hadn't been testified to in court. The sheriff had shared it with Cody, off the record, telling him he could use it in his spot that evening. The evidence had to do with the recovery of a hand-gun that had been traced to two separate murders from fifteen years earlier.

"We call 'em 'long-reach guns'," the sheriff had explained with a chuckle. "They reach out of the grave and point to someone somehow related to their murders. We don't usually get doubles, but this time was good. We've been after these two for a while, and now we can charge them with both murders and let them try to explain their way out of them."

"As in, where did they get the gun."

"Precisely. They're facing two counts of LWOP. Go to prison, die in prison." He chuckled again. "The irony is that these perps weren't even old enough to hold a gun when those murders were committed, but that won't stop the DA from throwing the book at them.

Cody quickly wrote up the exclusive information as "Channel 13 has learned..." and fifteen minutes after arriving back at the station, he was handing his script in to Belotti. The producer read through it.

"Hey, good stuff. How come you don't put in 'the district attorney told me' about the gun? It gives you more visibility."

"Yeah, I know, but I feel like we're a team. And Felice got those great shots of the perps. I don't think anyone else did."

Belotti shrugged. "Okay. I get it." He handed back the script. "Do it."

Cody did it, recording the script and giving it to Felice. He returned to his office and called Francie LeVillard.

"I hear you're trying to get yourself in trouble," she said when she took his call, seeing his number on her caller ID display. No preliminaries for her.

Cody laughed. "Word sure gets around the grapevine quickly in this market."

"It's a very short vine," she replied. "And yes, I can tell you what you need. Are you in a hurry? Do you have ten days?"

It was her questions that sent a chill up his spine. If he hadn't realized it before, he did now, that he had put his toe into treacherous waters. He didn't think it at all likely that word of his reporting interest would have come out of the sheriff's office, and he knew from Francie that her own security system was impeccable. Her good friend and sometime colleague, Ariane Chevasse, knew electronics and communications better than most everyone at the NSA and made sure that Francie was secure.

"Sooner than later, methinks," he answered without giving it further thought.

"How 'bout I pop by your house this evening?"

Startled, Cody replied, "Well that would be fine. Is that convenient for you, though? I mean..."

"I know what you mean. Yes, it's fine. Do you have any red wine or should I bring that too?"

"Yes on the red, and I'll have some food for you. When's good for you, Francie? Seven?"

"See you then."

"You know where I live?"

There was an pause at the other end. "Seven." Then the connection clicked off.

It was a few minutes before seven when Cody, who was standing at his kitchen counter drying some dishes, watched Francie get out of her Prius. She had parked it about fifty yards away, past Deki-san's house and across the street. He had recognized her car from dinner two nights previously. He saw that she didn't get out of her car immediately, and when she did, she stepped out smoothly so that she was ready to move if she had to, turning quickly to scan the full 365. Then she crossed the street toward Deki's house, paused briefly as if she were looking in the window, and continued to Cody's house where she didn't pause but walked directly up to the door. By then he had dried his hands and had gone to the door, opening it before she rang the bell. Actually, she hadn't even reached for the button. She had seen him through the window see her arrive.

"I can't stay long, but I didn't want you to feel naked," she said as she followed his gesture into the living room.

On the coffee table was an open bottle of Silver Oak Cabernet, two wine glasses, two plates, two damask napkins, and two trays of finger foods. "You stay as long as you like, Francie, but you have to make some inroads in the nibblies and the wine."

Having surveyed the set up as she walked in, she laughed, "My pleasure, Cody. How nice of you do to this."

She sat at one end of the dark red leather couch; Cody sat at the other and poured the wine. Francie opened her bag and pulled out two boxes and put them on the table next to her. Cody handed her a glass of wine and raised his glass to hers. "Pleasure before business," he said. The two clinked.

"Oh marvelous," she said, turning the bottle on the table so that she could read the label. "I forget how good some of the wine is coming from the Alexander Valley."

"The wine certainly is a good reason to live in California," Cody said.

"And the weather. I really love it here. I hope you do too. From what you've been through, you deserve to enjoy where you live. And find something to do that enriches you."

Cody looked at her thoughtfully. "What a lovely sentiment, Francie. Thank you." He held his glass up to her.

"Okay, let me tell you what I have for you." She opened the larger box and removed a small semi-automatic. "I cleaned it up for you. It's a Colt Mustang XSP. A pocket gun. Six-shot magazine. A .38 but its aluminum and stainless construction absorbs the kick. You can get a good group at 40 feet once you've shot ten mags."

Cody laughed.

"What?" she asked smiling back wanly, knowing the reason.

"To hear such talk coming from such an attractive woman, you'd only expect it in the movies."

She looked down at the gun and then up at Cody. The smile was gone. "I've had to shoot two people before they could shoot me, Cody. One had already fired once at me, but the woman who was his real target had jumped in front of me to take the bullet. She survived. He didn't. When she was in surgery a half-hour later, two of his friends broke into the OR and tried again. We stopped them dead. You need to know that this isn't a movie."

Cody cleared his throat. "Jeez. Sorry. I didn't mean to make light of this. I've got it now." He took a large sip of wine.

"I think you should go down to a friend of mine's place in Big Sur to shoot the gun in, rather than the range out at Laguna Seca. You'll be better off if no one thinks you're packing."

Cody quickly nodded his acceptance.

"I know you know something about guns. You want to know not only how this fires but why it might not. You should be able to take it apart and put it back together in the dark. That may sound crazy, but crazy is better than dead. I hope the only time you ever have to shoot is at a target but the world isn't what it used to be. I know you know that."

She handed him the gun. He felt its weight, and whistled at how surprisingly light it was. "Less than a pound," she told him.

He felt its heft in both hands, removed the magazine, pulled back the slide, checked the action of the safety, pointed it away, and pulled the trigger. He then pulled back the slide and pulled the trigger again. He changed hands and repeated all the maneuvers. He replaced the magazine, checked the slide action again, removed the magazine, unchambered the bullet, put it back in the magazine, and put the magazine back in the gun. Then he handed it back to Francie. "Nice trigger action," he reported favorably. "I like it. Thank you, Francie."

She put the gun back in the box, replaced the cover and put the box back on the table. She picked up her glass and took a careful sip.

"Mmm, good. Good. Okay, there's a loaded mag in the gun and two more mags in the box. Plus an ankle holster. I personally don't like them. I either have a pocket gun or a larger one on the back of my belt. You'll like the Colt, I think. Make friends with it. Until you know it, it will be more dangerous to you than useful, and useful means it could save your life. The other box," she nodded toward it on the table, "has four boxes of ACP, 200 rounds of 95-grain Mag-Tech. You can get more weight, but I don't think you need it, not if you know the gun and how to hit what you're aiming at."

"I'll go down this weekend, if that's all right."

"I'll check with Marlowe. He's there most weekends. Good guy. Then I'll get back to you to confirm." She took a piece of folded note paper from her bag, opened it, and then handed it to him. "His contact info and directions. Learn it, then destroy the paper, please."

Cody cocked his head at her but didn't say anything for a moment. "This is enough to scare a person," he said, aware that his voice was the very slightest bit tremulous.

"Good. You should be scared. Now. When you know what you're doing, especially when you know who you're dealing with, and your limits, the scary turns cold and you can operate. In a way it's like flying in weather. There are the FAA limitations on how low the clouds can be for you to land. Then there are your own personal limits. You need to know those cold. Never push your limits."

Cody shook his head. "I had no idea what I was getting into. This almost feels worse than Kandahar."

"In some ways it is. Here, some of the suits are more dangerous than the guys in prison stripes. I know you must have learned to trust your gut when you were over there. Trust it here. Your intuitive. Listen to it closely. Don't argue with it."

"No, I won't." He pulled his checkbook out of his pocket. "What's the tab for this, my friend?"

Francie smiled at him and waved him off. "I can't tell you how I got the gun but it didn't cost me anything. If you ever decide you don't want it, I'll take it back. You can give me a hundred for the bullets."

Cody looked at her to make sure that was right. She gave him a simple nod. He put away the checkbook and pulled cash out of his pocket. He peeled off the right amount and handed it to her. "I'm very grateful, Francie, on several levels."

"Good," she said, slipping the cash into a pocket. "Now let's dine."

Francie stayed for only a half-hour, during which time they ate most of the hors d'oeuvres and made a dead soldier of the Silver Oak. When he walked her to the door, she leaned forward to kiss him on both cheeks. "Don't put yourself at risk, Cody. No one is worth it. I'll call you about Marlowe's place. You're going to need that Colt. When you understand that, you'll be ready."

She didn't say ready for what. She didn't know, but Cody knew that she was right.

XVI

Before Cody went down to the private shooting range in Big Sur on Saturday morning, he learned how to disassemble and reassemble the gun. First in the light on the kitchen table, then in the dark in his lap; until he was confident he could do it even under pressure. He loaded and unloaded the three magazines several times to make sure the action was smooth. And at the appointed time, he drove down Highway One, turning onto the Old Coast Road just before the Bixby Bridge, and continuing several miles until he saw the appropriate landmarks Francie had given him.

"You're the new guy at 13," said the burly, bearded man of a sixty-plus indeterminate age, shaking Cody's hand. "I saw you. Pretty good. Better than the rest of the market. I hope you last. Come on," and he led him behind his double-wide into a meadow backed by a berm with some torso targets attached to wooden frames standing in front of the dirt.

"It's all yours. I'll be inside if you need anything. I'll come out when the firing's stopped for awhile." With that he clapped Cody on his shoulder and left him to shoot. And that's what Cody did.

As he reported to Francie when he got home, he shot off each of the magazines five times. Only once had he had to clear the breech. Otherwise everything had functioned as it should. On his way home he'd picked up another couple of boxes of cartridges and a gun cleaning kit.

"How'd the targets fare?" Francie asked.

"They got hurt where they were supposed to. I was always within the bottle. Single shots and doubles. The gun feels like she's mine."

"She?"

"Yeah. We're real close."

Francie laughed, "Good for you, Cody. I hope you never have to use her for why you have her, but she will take care of you if you do."

"Much appreciated again, Francie. I hope you'll maybe let me take you to dinner next week."

"That would be nice, " she said. "Let's talk at the beginning of the week when we have a better handle on our schedules."

"Plan," Cody said simply, and "Be well."

"You too, Cody. You too," she said and clicked off.

On Monday morning, Cody thought he might hold off carrying the Colt until he was actually investigating the goings-on at Soledad, but he decided that he was just resisting the idea of packing, so he put the holster on the inside of his left leg above his ankle. He wasn't going to get a fast play off that position, but for simply being at the office and doing daily business until he poked the sleeping Soledad tiger, it would be within reasonable reach. If he thought things might get dicey, he'd move it to a pocket. He was pleased and surprised how quickly he stopped noticing it on his leg.

When he got to the office, Belotti told him that Burgess wanted to see him. The reporter put his things on his desk and went upstairs. He knocked on the open door of the news director's office. Instead of inviting him in, Burgess lifted his huge bulk out of his chair, and with a "come on" led Cody to the station manager's office where Big Don welcomed his reporter with a big warm smile and gesture for him to sit down in one of the two chairs in front of his desk. Burgess remained standing with his back against the wall behind the station manager; neither chair would have put up with his weight.

"Cody," the station manager opened, "you had one helluva first week, and I have to say, I'm glad you've come on board."

"Why thank you, sir," Cody said, glancing up to find a noncommital expression – that was a generous interpretation – on the face of the news director.

"I know talent when I see it, and I want to make the most of it. I think we want Ron and Lara in the field where they can use their reporting skills best, and put you at the anchor desk, solo. What do you think of that?" he asked beaming.

Cody was shocked but only mildly since this was the 125th market. A number of responses zipped through his mind, none of them appropriate; for instance, "Replace Jabba the Hutt with me as news director."

Big Don held up his big hand. "I know what you're thinking, Cody, that you should get a boost in pay." He winced, "But you're already under contract and making more than anyone else in the station, except for me." That produced a big laugh which found no echo – not even a smile – on the face of the news director.

Cody shook his head. "I was just taking in your offer," he said. "I am honored that you would consider me for the position." He paused for effect. "I would be glad to anchor for you, sir," he said with a triumphant smile. He stood and reached his hand across the desk to seal the deal. Big Don got up, too, and shook his new anchorman's hand with enthusiasm.

The two men regained their chairs. "When do you want this to start?" Cody asked.

"Why, tonight." He swivelled to check with his news director who gave him a wan smile. Of course, Burgess had known what was coming and when, but even smart politics couldn't stretch his smile into a lie.

"Okay," Cody nodded. "I'd like to ask one thing." He thought, and amended, "Two things."

The corners of Big Don's smile dropped just a touch. He'd already said there was no more money; what could this man possibly want? He found out.

"One is that I want to format and write the newscast myself. That would give Nick more time to manage assignments and work with the reporters."

Big Don pointedly ignored the incommoded wheeze behind him, thought but for three seconds. "We can give that a try. What's the other thing?"

"I think we would give the news a more formal look if I delivered the news from behind a working desk. It would distinguish 13 from the sparkling neon-news they do in Salinas. It would show that we are about real news, not just pretty faces; giving the audience what they need to know instead of make-nice reporting to keep them happy."

Big Don squinted at Cody for a good ten seconds, and when he spoke, his tone had changed. He was no longer the glad-handing corporate executive. He had immediately understood the distinction with the competition and saw the potential to move his station forward. "I like it. I like it," he said thoughtfully, and a moment later he added, "we may not get the numbers they do, but we can sure attract the cream demos." He slapped his hand on his desk. "Yes, Cody, let's go for it."

It was probably the most excited Big Don had been in years. He had someone who could produce quality ratings that would increase advertising revenues which would garner the attention of corporate. Not that he wanted to move to another Enlaw station. Not Toledo or Dubuque. Not Albuquerque or number 26 Indianapolis. He liked Monterey. He was known and respected in the community. He liked the welcome he got at his Rotary meetings on Wednesdays. And most important, his wife – his job security – was happy. If Cody Howard could help solidify that for him, well, bang-zoom, Cody was his guy.

He turned slightly and said over his shoulder to his news director, "Herb, make this happen. Send someone over to Office Depot for a nice desk. Spend a coupla hundred dollars. Explain things to Ron and Lara, and to Nick. And call Rudy at home, tell him what we're doing. Get him in here early to adjust the lighting. He should like this a lot better, one anchor instead of two. A much easier show."

Burgess mumbled something like "yessir" although it might have been heard as "woe is me," and he shuffled around the desk and out the door. Cody stood up as the news director passed him. He faced Big Don. "Thank you. I won't let you down," he said, then he turned and followed Burgess out the door. As they walked down the hall, Cody offered, "I know you have a lot to do now, Herb. I can go pick up the desk."

The news director stopped at the entrance to his office and turned to face the new anchorman. He opened his mouth to respond but before he could speak, Cody said, "Listen Herb, I know this wasn't your idea, but I'm going to do a good job. The ratings will go up, and you as news director will get credit for it. So let's make this work."

Burgess looked at him with malevolent eyes. "Fuck you," he said.

Cody couldn't help himself. He laughed and said, "I'll go get the desk."

XVII

It would have been grand if the early Channel 13 news had gone off without a hitch, but it would have been a first. A tape report wouldn't play back properly, so their new anchorman apologized and explained to the audience the gist of what the reporter would have told them. Also, Herb Burgess came down to the newsroom to watch and stood in front of one of the key lights. He probably didn't do it on purpose. When the late show aired, those two issues had been resolved. The tape report had been re-edited, and Burgess had gone home hours earlier. But the sports guy forgot to put on his microphone, and the weather lady mispronounced Des Moines, enunciating both esses clearly.

That said, the newscast was demonstrably better than it maybe ever had been. The news was formatted differently, with headlines of the most important stories at the top, and then segments for local, national, and world news following. Also, there was no banter between the news anchor and the sports and weather people. They didn't want to talk to Cody anyway, since he'd cut sports thirty seconds to two-and-a-half-minutes and the weather to a minute-and-a-half. That gave him more time for news, which he used by voicing over two clips from the CBS Evening News and airing a tense exchange on Capitol Hill between a stubborn Pentagon general and a confused Congressman.

So while not everyone was happy, Cody could see in the faces in the newsroom the next day that they knew and understood the changes. Otherwise, the response to his debut was greeted positively, from people he knew, and from others he didn't. "Who'd have thunk?" he said to himself aloud, thinking back just a few weeks earlier.

Tuesday evening's newscasts went relatively smoothly, as did the rest of the week. By Friday, Cody had received invitations to speak before two service organizations, and the vice chancellor at CSUMB called to find out if he'd be interested in teaching a course at the local university. Cody accepted the two speaking invitations – they would be a great way to increase the audience for the newscasts – and he put the teaching idea on hold.

His days were already long enough as he was, by his own choice, writing the newscasts. It wasn't that there was an immense number of stories to write, so much as he had to stay on top of the news and make sure he got all of the important news in. Plus he read and provided guidance to the reporters on their scripts. He was pleased that his reception to his new role had been more easily accepted than it might have been. The reporters, and the rest of the news staff, had a renewed sense of purpose. And they knew that a successful newscast would be good for them all. It raised their standards, if not immediately their paychecks, and for those looking to advance to higher markets, it meant better quality reporting on their demo tapes.

But the full schedule meant that Cody had to reschedule his promised, and desired, dinner with Francie LeVillard. She was free that Saturday night, and suggested that they meet at Little Napoli. She would make reservations for seven. She was already at the restaurant, talking with the owner, when Cody arrived. She introduced him to Rich Pèpe, a New Jersey transplant, highly-successful restauranteur, and very-visible figure in Carmel. Cody hadn't yet drilled down into the dramatis personae of Carmel-by-the-Sea to be fully aware of Pèpe but he'd come across the man's name in reading about the move to unseat the city manager.

"Hey," he said to Cody, "I saw your news last night. I never watched your station in maybe twenty years, it's been so long. But I heard it was new, and I gotta say, you were good. Like they did it in New York before they got all chatty-cathy like *Saturday Night Live*. I like that you talk about the real news, in the country and the world. Not just the local stuff."

"Why thank you, Mr. Pèpe...."

"No, Mr. Pèpe. Just Pèpe, or call me Rich. And like I was saying, or I didn't yet, but I was telling my wife 'cause she was watching too and liked you a lot, I think maybe I should put some advertising on your station. I mean, you're gonna be attracting the smart people, and smart people have money. They can afford to eat good...what we serve here."

"Rich, that would be great. I know we're not going to beat the competition for numbers, but we can certainly draw an overall smarter viewership. Thank you."

"Hey, yeah, and not only me. I'll talk to other businesses, too. They should get behind you. The ones that cater to a high-end clientele." Before Cody could respond with more thank-you's he added, "You do good, we do good. It's the way it works." Then he turned to Francie. He took her hand and brought it to his lips. "We don't see enough of you, Francie. You need to come to town more."

"Pèp, you're absolutely right. And now that I'll be seeing your restaurants on the news, I'll remember to eat here more often."

"Good girl, you." He turned and beckoned the maitre d'. "Alonzo, they have my table, next to the patio, right? You take care of them yourself."

"Of course, Pèpe," the maitre d' said, and he ushered the couple to a corner in the back room. Their table was by a large window that looked out onto a courtyard, brightly lit with colored lights. It was too cool still for outdoor dining, so this was as close as they could get.

"I often have the eggplant parmigiana, but the veal piccata is excellent, and you have to at least try his Alfredo sauce. It comes on *tagliatelle* with my eggplant. I'll give you a taste."

"Thank goodness I brought an appetite."

"There are many restaurants on The Peninsula, some of them surviving on the tourist dollar. Others cater more to the locals to be their repeat customers. Pèpe gets both, with the locals being smart about when to avoid the crowds."

"What an interesting guy. There's something different about the people from the east coast, isn't there?"

"You've noticed that already. Yes. More of an edge. Not unpleasant, but sharper."

"Are there are a lot of east coast people here in Carmel, and on The Peninsula?"

"Enough to make it interesting," Francie replied with a laugh. "And some wonderful four-generation Californians, too."

"I didn't mean..."

"No, of course not. There are some fascinating nuances about the people here, especially here in Carmel. A unique group of artists, retirees, and others who love the climate and the atmosphere. Some very bright folks. A number of widows. And some singles like us."

"There is something in the air, isn't there? It's different here."

Francie nodded. Alonzo arrived with a plate of antipasto and a basket of steaming fresh bread. He was accompanied by the sommelier who had a bottle of Pèpe "Vesuvio." "It is a blend of Cabernet, Merlot and Syrah," he explained. "He bottles only 500 cases a year. He asks that you do him the honor of tasting it."

"Delighted," Francie said.

The sommelier opened the bottle, examined the cork, and put it down on the table. "It will be ready in time for your dinner. In the meantime," he turned and took a silver tray with a bottle and two glasses on it from a busboy behind him, "You will please enjoy this Chianti, which Pèpe discovered at a small vineyard near Paso Robles." He put the glasses on the table before them and poured a half-glass into each. "Enjoy," he said, bowing slightly and leaving them.

Francie raised her glass to Cody. "It's wonderful to have friends who have restaurants." They clinked glasses and drank. "Pèpe does know what he's doing."

"Delicious," Cody agreed. They broke bread and leisurely tasted the variety of meats, cheeses, and vegetables on the antipasto plate. It was almost twenty minutes, when they'd done justice to the appetizers, and Alonzo arrived with their meals and then poured the wine. "Pèpe asked me to tell you that you should not feel rushed, and that you might save some room for the tiramisu."

They dined slowly, sharing tastes and delighted "ahs." The conversation was a stern counterpoint to the food. Francie provided important background and a couple of critical contacts for Cody's pursuit of the Soledad prison story. She was personally aware of two inmates who had been murdered inside the prison walls by other inmates on the orders of one of the imprisoned crime bosses.

"He did it for me, actually," she said with a grimace on her face. "I can't tell you about my connection, but I can tell you what happened." Then she related how a friend of hers, an important friend, had been murdered by a young gang-banger wannabe who mistook him for someone else. "A good perfectly innocent man was assassinated by this kid who was trying to make his bones with the gang. The other guy they killed was the one who ordered the hit, but on the real target."

"It was done for you?" Cody asked, unable to mask his incredulity.

Francie nodded soberly. "Not at my request, of course." She sighed. "I need to tell you the whole story." And she did.

"Up close and personal," Cody commented when she was finished.

"Very close, very personal," she replied in a soft voice.

"I'm sorry, Francie. When did this happen?"

"Last year." She shook her head sharply as if trying to loosen the memory. "I never thought it would have this kind of hold on me."

"Yeah, it's unfortunate that the mind traps those pieces and we can't get free of them."

She nodded, cleared her throat, and then said, "Here's who you need to talk to." She handed him a piece of otherwise blank paper with two names and phone numbers. "Gonzalez is the new name of a former guard who escaped with his life, just barely. He's living in Central America. He agreed to tell you his story if you call from a pre-paid phone and then destroy it. His number will only be good for" – she looked at her watch – "another 42 hours.

"And Jack Early is an attorney. Someone planted a large bag of coke – packaged for sale, not personal use – in his car while he was meeting with DofC – Department of Corrections – officials in Sacramento. He can fill you in on the details."

"Jesus, doesn't anyone care about this? People who could do something?"

Francie stared at him, her fork with a bite of pasta poised a few inches from her mouth. She put the fork back on the plate, daintily wiped her mouth with her napkin, and returned it to her lap. "You have your Colt with you?" She asked in a lowered voice.

Cody casually looked through the window and then all around them in the restaurant. "Yes. I thought about not bringing it since I wasn't going to work on this story until next week. And this is just a quiet dinner."

"But?"

"But since I shot down at Marlowe's, I thought it was important that I get comfortable with having it on my person every time I leave the house."

"Very smart. Again, I hope you never need it, but as they said in the American Express commercial, 'Don't leave home without it.' And for that matter, know where it is at all times in the house. I don't mean to scare you, Cody, and it's not too late for you to come to your senses and just be the best anchor this market has ever seen, but when you talk to Gonzalez and Early, you'll know why I'm talking this way. And you'll have stepped in it."

XVIII

Cody found himself walking in from the parking lot Monday morning catching up with Manda Viscaino, KMTY's sales manager. It wasn't difficult to catch up to her. She was, as the ads say, plus-size, and didn't move very quickly. On another day, Cody might have dawdled since he thought little of the sales operation and had nothing to say. But this day he did. "Good morning, Manda. How are you this bright Monday?"

She looked at him askance, then at the sky, then at him. "It's cloudy."

"Ah, yes, but our spirits are bright, aren't they?"

She walked but now with her eyes pointed over her bulk at her next steps. In fairness, she wasn't unattractive but for her size, which did little to lighten her spirits. Fat people are not always jolly.

"Well, I may have some good news for you. Give Rich Pèpe a call. I had dinner at Little Napoli on Saturday night, and I think he is interested in advertising on the news."

The woman shook her head. "No, he doesn't advertise on our station. I don't think he does any television."

"Apparently he's changed his mind?"

She looked up at him. "Really?"

"Really. And he may round up some other advertisers for us."

"Why?"

"He likes what we are doing with the news, Manda." He put some force behind this last statement, and bit his lip before he might have asked her if she had seen the new newscasts and what she thought of them.

"Does that mean splitting commissions? Including his referrals?"

Cody had to stifle a laugh. "Uh, no." He might have added, just Pèpe's buys, but he thought he would leave her hanging and see what she did with them. It wasn't about the money, which wouldn't be a huge amount, but the wakefulness. The news staff was already getting on board. Now the rest of the station had to follow.

"Okay," she relented. "I'll call him."

No "thank-you" or "well done" from her. Disappointing but not unexpected. They had reached the main door. Cody stepped ahead and opened the door for her to enter first. She forced a smile and headed for the elevator. Cody walked through to the newsroom. He checked in with Nick Belotti to learn about the day's local coverage, and then check the major news sites online to see what had changed since he'd been online a half-hour earlier.

When there was nothing requiring his immediate attention, he told the assignment manager he had an errand, and drove out to the large shopping mall in Salinas. He parked at the outer perimeter of the lot and took out his pre-paid phone. He'd memorized the names and numbers Francie had given him and destroyed the paper. He would properly dispose of the phone when his work was done.

The first call he made was to Gonzalez. As Francie had instructed, when the phone was answered with a curt "Si," he said simply, "Our friend told you I'd call." There was silence on the other end. Then a more relaxed voice told me, "She is a good friend. She saved my life, okay. So she said you wanted to know what happened to me, and just to tell you the facts. You ready?"

"Yes, and thank you."

For the next fifteen minutes, Gonzalez told Cody in vivid detail how he'd been a guard at Soledad for three years starting six years ago. For the last three years, he'd been hiding out with a new identity, always looking over his shoulder. He wouldn't provide any details of his current circumstances since he didn't want to give any clues to the people who were still looking for him. They would always be looking for him; that's the way they were.

He was okay at Soledad for a couple of years. He had known what he was getting into there. A couple of the guards had been his friends; that's how he got his job. What they hadn't told him about was the degree of corruption. It was everywhere in the prison system, probably in every state, but it was especially bad in California because the state was so big, and because there were a lot of Latinos. No, not Mexican-Americans, he made it clear. Almost all the Latinos were either illegal aliens or they were just criminals who were working this side of the border.

Almost all the prisoners were behind bars for drug-related crimes. Some selling, some smuggling, but most of those at Soledad were there because they were gang leaders or enforcers. Probably half were in for violent crimes. Most of the other half had done violent crimes but had pleaded down to something else so they might have a chance of getting back on the street before all their hair was grey.

Gonzalez had been successful for the first two years just keeping his head down and doing his job. He had good six-month evaluations, including fewer than average complaints by inmates. But then one of the lieutenants began to grow wary of him. Unlike all of the other guards, Gonzalez didn't lie on his time card. He only put down the hours that he worked, instead of adding five to ten hours of overtime as was the norm. One of the lieutenants raised the issue with some of the other guards, wondering aloud if Gonzalez might not be a mole for the Department of Corrections Investigation Bureau.

Feeling that they would be more vulnerable if he wasn't dirty too, some of the more egregious offenders started pressuring Gonzalez to put in for extra time. He refused. Then they tried to force him into violations of the rule book. In several instances, they tried to coerce inmates into lying about his treatment of them. Ironically, they refused, even though it cost them. They had a code of honor that superceded that of the prison authority.

Finally they had him reassigned to the B ward where the mental cases were warehoused.

Gonzalez knew that he wouldn't survive the posting. The only guards that did were borderline crazy themselves. They were more violent than the inmates and took out their problems on those in their charge. By the end of the first week in B ward, he had been involved in several altercations with inmates, two of them directly instigated by his fellow guards. At the end of the week, he went on sick leave and put in for a transfer to another prison.

The request never left Soledad, but Gonzalez didn't find out until he called a friend in Sacramento to learn the status of his request. When someone in Sacramento called down to Soledad to find out what had happened to the transfer request, there was an explosion. The lieutenant who had caused all the fuss said it was proof that Gonzalez was a mole. They sent information through the grapevine that he was collecting evidence against one of the cartel's top men in Soledad that would send him to the even worse hell at Pelican Bay.

For the cartel, that was unacceptable. They arranged for Gonzalez to be framed in the death of an inmate, but first they decided to soften him up. They had one of their people on the outside slash his tires which he wouldn't discover until just before he was to leave for work. Then that night, they had someone pick a fight with him at his pizza joint at the mouth of Carmel Valley. The plan went bad when Gonzalez got the better of the bigger man who attacked him, and in a fury, lying on the floor, the man pulled a gun.

As it happened Francie LeVillard also liked the food at that particular restaurant and had walked in to pick up her favorite pizza. She was standing behind the man on the floor when he pulled out the gun. Without thinking, she stomped on his elbow, shattering several bones, and sending the gun skittering across the floor to land at Gonzalez' feet. He picked up the gun, walked over to the man, and aimed it at his groin. The man's cries of pain turned to a sobbing plea for mercy.

"Who put you up to this, *mierda*?"

"Nobody, nobody. I did it."

Gonzalez cocked the hammer. "I didn't hear you."

"No, no, don't ," the big man pleaded. "They'll kill me."

"No they won't," Gonzalez told him. "After I blow away your balls, while you're writhing around on the floor screaming, then I'm going to put one in your gut, and you'll feel the acid burning you inside out. You'll be begging me to put you out of your misery."

"Don't shoot, don't shoot. I'll tell you."

Gonzalez aimed a vicious kick at the man's solar plexus, drawing sharp cries of pain. The sound of sirens cut through his plaint. "If you don't tell me quick, the cops are gonna find you dead, *cabrón*. And if you didn't know it, I've got a badge. But you did know it, didn't you?" With a rapid strike, Gonzalez poked the muzzle of the gun hard into the man's gut.

"Okay, okay, don't shoot. It was *El Caimán*. He told me."

"He told you what?"

"To fight with you. To hurt you."

"How much did he pay you?"

There was a moment's hesitation and the sirens were getting louder. Gonzalez kicked him again, though not as hard. He didn't need to.

"Two hundred. Two hundred. I'll give it to you."

"Where's the money?"

Reluctantly, "In my pocket."

"Which pocket, stupido?"

"Pants...front." He couldn't use his right hand since his elbow was in pieces.

"Ma'am," he said to Francie, "would you please reach into his pocket and remove the money?"

"Are you are a cop?"

"Prison guard. Someone inside was planning to kill me."

Francie hesitated only a second. She quickly relieved the man of a wad of cash and stepped back. "What do you want me to do with it?"

"Give a hundred to Mark behind the counter, and you can keep the rest."

"I don't want his money."

"Okay, then give it to me. I've got to get out of here."

That's what she did. He didn't count it there. He slipped the gun in his pocket and the cash in another, and headed for the door. He looked outside and then back at Francie. "Thank you, lady. You saved my life." With that he left. He circled around the building getting back to his car just as the police were pulling up out front. He waited until they had gone inside and then unobtrusively exited the parking lot.

Gonzalez calculated that he had enough time to get home long before the man with the smashed elbow would be allowed to make a phone call. He drove to his apartment, scanning the area carefully before he entered. When he deemed it safe, he moved quickly to take his clothes, computer, and valuables. Then he drove back to the Monterey Regional Airport, parked his car in the long-term lot, rented a car, transferred all of his things to the new wheels, and headed out of town. He drove to Sacramento. The next morning, he met surreptitiously with his friend from the prisons department and told him what happened. He said he was going to disappear and no one was going to find him.

And that's what he did. He easily bought a new identity, got a new computer, new phone, new bank account, and headed to a place where he would blend in with the local population without generating questions. After he had been settled for a while, he made contact with Francie LeVillard whose name he had gotten from the local news coverage online. He thanked her again for saving his life and gave her a special code to get in touch with him if the need arose.

He later learned that Francie had informed *El Caimán* about how he had been set up by the local prison officials, specifically the lieutenant who had it in for Gonzalez. She had contacted Gonzalez to let him know that there was no longer a price on his head. While he believed her and was grateful for her efforts, he didn't believe he was safe. Everyone hears when the sentence is imposed, but not everyone hears when it's lifted. He decided to stay in hiding, since his new life was better than working as a prison guard.

That was the last he had heard from her until a few days ago. Gonzalez was telling Cody his story in appreciation for what Francie had done for him, first saving his life, and then taking at least some of the heat off. But, he added, he didn't have any hope that Cody could make a difference.

"Thank you for telling me your story. I'll tell Francie. And I'll see what I can do to fix the situation at the prison."

"Hey, man, I appreciate what you're saying, but if you want some good advice – if you want to stay alive – I tell you, write your story and send it to the governor or the president or someone. Then get out of the line of fire. It's not worth it. It's not going to change. They can't kill enough of them, the guards and the inmates, to make a difference." With that the line went dead.

Cody turned off the phone and wearing rubber gloves, he wiped it clean of fingerprints. Then he opened the car door, put the phone on the pavement, and then smashed it with the heel of his shoe. Content that there was nothing recoverable from it, he put the remains in his half-cup of coffee. He drove over to a waste hauler and carefully pushed the cup down into one of the corners.

Then he drove to the other side of Salinas and parked in the corner of a strip mall parking lot to call the attorney, Jack Early. It turned out to be a shorter call, and just as not sweet.

Early had represented two men who had pled to lesser charges in exchange for lesser sentences if they turned state's evidence. Also, part of the deal was that they be imprisoned in a facility far away from the reach of the cartel against whom they testified. This was back in the days when the cartels weren't as well understood. The truth, they belatedly discovered, was that there were no prisons beyond the cartels' reach. Even at a federal pen like the one at Leavenworth, Kansas. That was where the men were sent. They lived only a week. Then they were found in their bunks with their throats slit. And to make sure that there was no question about what was the reason behind the executions, both had their mouths filled with cocaine before they were killed.

Early was furious. He drove to Sacramento to confront the head of the Department of Corrections. It was pointless, of course, since Leavenworth was a federal prison; what could the man have done? He was at least sympathetic toward Early, letting him vent for a good fifteen minutes before telling him he could do nothing more. Early departed, deflated and hurting. He got into his car and was about to drive away when he saw flashing red lights and sheriff's deputies around his car with guns drawn and pointed at him. He froze and did exactly what they ordered him to do. That consisted of showing his hands and getting out of the car very slowly. Then they had him put his hands on the roof of his car. He was frisked very carefully – almost intimately, he told Cody – as the car was searched.

"You had to have guessed, didn't you? They opened the trunk and what did they find? Cocaine. A few pounds. Nicely wrapped for street dealers to cut and sell. They had gotten an anonymous telephone tip. Surprise, surprise."

Early was arrested, of course, charged, and had to spend a night in jail before a grateful client put up the seven-figure bail, enabling the attorney to be freed the next morning. The charges were dropped two days later when the absurdity of the situation was explored by healthier minds. For one thing, while there were no fingerprints on the packages of cocaine, there were on the trunk. They were not Early's. In fact they correlated in the federal data base with not one but two convicted felons who had been paroled from drug time at a state penitentiary in Louisiana. Warrants were issued for their arrest.

"That wasn't the end of it," Early told Cody. "The frickin' ethics committee of the frickin' California Bar Association had to investigate. They have to do that any time an attorney is arrested on felony charges. It took them three months to come to the conclusion that there wasn't a case against me." He chuckled. "I was sooo close to telling them to go you-know-what-to-themselves and find myself another profession. One more noble, like selling sub-prime bundles for Goldman Sachs."

He cleared his throat. "Of course, the question arises, who put the stuff in the trunk of my car? Was it the cops or the robbers? They both have access to all the cocaine they want. What they left in my trunk was not even a drop in the bucket. The cops knew where I was headed that day, but ya gotta know that the robbers have the state's operation infiltrated six ways to breakfast. And it's not like I'm hard to find. So either of them could have set me up."

"I'm glad you were cleared. Have you kept your head down since?"

With a sullen tone in his voice the attorney replied, "I never thought much of martyrdom. Especially my own. I thought I was sacrificing enough by representing prisoners, as noble as that was, considering their plight. But I got to thinking that there were plenty of areas of law that were noble that were not life-threatening, and that were also not about defending sub-prime mortgage brokers. So I've shifted into environmental law. Oh yeah, there are some nasty people who can get angry at you, but they have more to risk. At least that's how I rationalize it to myself. Plus, between you and me and the lamp post, I found a great lady, and I would never do anything to put her at risk. Greedy developers have their limits. They don't murder girlfriends."

"I'm glad you found someone. It makes all the difference in the world. I don't think I would be pursuing this story if I weren't alone." He sighed. "Frankly, I'd rather have someone in my life, but that's another issue. Jack, can I call you back if I have more questions?"

There was a demonstrable silence on the other end of the line. "I'd rather you didn't, but if you really needed something you couldn't get anywhere else, I guess. For Francie. Tell her I said 'hi,' would you?"

"Will do. And thank you."

"Yeah. Take care."

Cody clicked off the call. He didn't have any more coffee, so he did an extra good job smashing the phone. On the way back to the office, he dropped what was left of it in an oil recycling tank at a gas station.

XIX

When Cody got home that night, he was surprised to see lights on in Deki-san's house. His neighbor was usually in bed early. He was more surprised when he saw the man walking up his driveway as Cody got out of his car.

"You're up late, my esteemed friend," he said, shutting the garage door and gesturing for Deki to go to the front door. Cody unlocked it and directed the man toward the living room. When he declined an offer of food or drink, Cody followed him in.

"I thought you should know but I didn't want to tell you on the telephone at your work."

That was an inauspicious opening. It got worse.

"There were two men in a car parked across the street, looking at your house."

"Oh, no," Cody moaned, realizing that he had already acquired the attention of the black hats. Probably from his call to Jack Early. He wondered if they had heard everything they'd said, or just knew of the contact.

"You have stirred up the dregs from the bottom of the pot." There was an edge in his voice but Cody knew it was not about him but the situation. "You should call your friend the detective. She has someone who can properly secure your house."

"I'll call her first thing in the morning."

"You call her now. She will understand."

Cody looked at him for a moment, further unsettled by the force in his voice. He picked up his phone and called Francie on the private number she had given him. She answered on the first ring.

"Sorry for calling so late."

"Call anytime, Cody. I was up watching your newscast. Good job, again. What's up?"

"Deki-san said he saw two men in a car parked across the street, watching my house today."

"You made your calls, didn't you? To the man with the time limit and the other man?"

"Yes. On different disposable phones."

"Good."

"Good?"

"Yes. I'm sure Deki-san told you that you'd roiled the waters."

"He didn't put it quite that way, but that was certainly the meaning."

"And didn't you know what was going to be the result? It's why you were practicing, you know, down south."

"Yes, I knew, I guess I hadn't realized it would happen so quickly."

"Okay, sit still. I'm going to call my friend. I'll call you right back."

It was less than a minute that the phone rang. "Make some coffee, or break out a decent bottle of wine. We're on our way over. Tell Deki-san."

It wasn't thirty minutes later that two cars pulled up in front of his house. Cody opened the door. When he saw Francie pulling boxes out of the back seat of the other car, he went down to help. There he met a woman who might have been her sister, or more likely a cousin, an inch taller, a little more auburn in her hair, but her energy was very much like Francie's; confident but not smug.

"Cody, this is my best friend and often colleague, Ariane Chevasse. She is a top spook who does freelancing for the government when they get stuck. She also knows all about the latest electronics, more than the NSA. She knew Edward Snowden."

Cody's arms were filled with several boxes so he was unable to shake hands. "Thank you for coming over at this ridiculous hour."

"*Mon ami,* with these people you're dealing with, any delay would be foolhardy."

They walked up the path to the front door and entered. "I think put everything in the kitchen," Ariane said, taking easy charge. "I will survey the whole house, but I think we found out what we needed online."

"Online?" Cody asked.

"We looked at photographs and blueprints of your house where they were filed by the architect," Francie explained. "We'll check to see if there was any updating that needs to be considered." She turned and walked toward the living room where Deki-san stood up from their arrival. She stopped six feet away from him, clapped her hands together silently in front of her chest and bowed over them. He bowed to her.

"Thank you, Deki-san, for looking after our important new friend."

"It is as it must be."

"I think you know, Ariane. She visited your illustrious restaurant with me more than once."

"Of course," he said, turning slightly to face her directly. "It refreshes the soul to be in your presence again."

"I am honored, Deki-san."

"All right, Ariane and I are going to look around. I think we know what's what. The installation won't take more than an hour or so, isn't that right?"

"From what we could see online, *c'est ça.*"

"Tea or wine?" Francie asked her.

"I think tea," came the reply.

Francie nodded to Cody, and the two women started their examination of his house. Cody filled a kettle and put light to a burner. Then he returned to the living room. Deki was sitting on the edge of the couch, his back comfortably erect; that's the way he always sat. Cody sat in a chair across from him.

"I feel I've walked on the set in the middle of a play, and I have no idea of the plot or the other characters."

Deki smiled. "Such is the way of life, isn't it? Instead of focusing on who we are, we think about our surroundings. How will we know what is our role if we don't know who we are? But the true nature is that once we have an idea about our own self, we won't have to act."

There had been a time when Cody would have, at least privately, scoffed at such thinking, but he'd seen too much now to dismiss it. And perhaps in just his transition of the past month, he'd paradoxically discovered the voice inside that could not only hear but listen. He laughed lightly. "I feel like such an amateur. I'm not used to relying on others, especially when they know so much that I need to know."

"How does it make you feel?"

"Grateful, but off balance. Or should I say, off balance, but grateful."

"Good. Being receptive will save your life."

"That's what makes me feel off balance."

"It is always a lesson, when you feel out of yourself. The Chinese calligraphy for the English word *crisis* is comprised of two symbols. The first means *danger* and the second means *opportunity*."

"The danger," the reporter said, "is that my life is threatened. The opportunity to nullify the threat comes about because you and Francie, and now Ariane, are watching out for me. For some reason. I think that's where I get stuck, Deki-san. It seems that you know the script, and I'm just bumbling along, lucky not to be killed."

"It is never about luck. Luck is a word invented to explain what people don't understand. It may be that the universe is perceived as chaotic, but that is because its order doesn't fit into the understanding of lower human reason. It is why when some tragic event occurs to children or other innocents, religious people wrap themselves in the thin cloak of 'It's God's will.'"

"I can appreciate the idea that there is no such thing as luck. It's just what happens. But as far as people explaining away indefensible events as 'God's will,' surely that's little different from saying the universe is orderly."

"It's entirely different. One is seeking explanations. The other isn't. There is always a series of circumstances that leads to a moment in time, to an event. That's the only explanation there is. There is no reasoning to why this child was molested by a priest or this family died in a car wreck. Just facts that preceded the events. It is like people who need to imbue a shark with the purpose to murder. The shark is eating to survive. It is the most primitive instinct. There is no morality involved. There is no murderous intent."

Cody was silent for a long moment and he digested the man's ideas. "And we anthropomorphize the shark, giving it human emotions, for what purpose?"

Deki smiled. "To provide a target object for their fear. Civilization is at a stage of living life in conflict. There is the presumption of struggle. It is part of our language. We have to 'earn' a living. But even for the wealthy, they create problems in their life that they have to face. The dressmaker won't have the $50,000 gown ready for the charity ball. The private jet couldn't get clearance because of bad weather. The accountant could only write off half of the vacation. Conflict is what defines us, whether it is real or manufactured."

"I understand what you are saying, Deki-san, and it certainly makes sense. I don't know why it didn't occur to me earlier in my life. You say it is a stage. What comes next? How do we get there?"

"Ah, now you have taken the big step, Cody-san."

"Cody-san. I like that," he laughed. "Okay, what is the big step?"

Deki smiled at him. "The next step is to truly live in the moment. Struggle occurs only with the past and the future. We obsess about what has happened to us and what will happen to us. We throw ourselves out of balance. No wonder we sense so much chaos. When we learn to live in the moment, the struggle, the conflict, and the chaos go away. We don't spend time or attention tilting at windmills. We engage what is, not what was or what will be."

"When do we get to this stage? And how?"

Deki looked down at his hands folded lightly in his lap for perhaps a minute. Softly he said, "We are there now."

Suddenly the kettle began to whistle, and at the same time the women came in through the front door. Cody had been so engrossed in his conversation he hadn't noticed them come down the stairs and exit through the garage door.

"Oh good, tea," Francie said and she and Ariane headed to the kitchen. "Jasmine, Deki-san."

"Most excellent," he replied.

"I don't think I have jasmine, Francie. I'm afraid I only have English breakfast and some Sleepytime."

"You have jasmine, Cody. You carried it in from the car for us."

"Aren't we clever?" Cody responded.

"Yes, we are. Now you do have a pitcher, don't you?"

Cody pulled down a teapot in a lovely Delft blue design. "Will this do?"

"I'm impressed," Francie said.

"I picked it up at an auction in Amherst, Massachusetts. There were magnificent estate sales from the whalers of the 19th century who had their summer homes in the area. They traveled the world and came home with wonderful pieces."

"I noticed a number of interesting pieces in your house, Cody," said Ariane. "Both furniture and art. You have very eclectic taste. And very good," she added quickly and laughed. "At least, I share it."

"Thank you, Ariane. A lot of it I got from those auctions. My parents lived in Northampton at the time. My father taught psychology at Smith. I would drive up for the weekend when he spotted some particularly good estates being auctioned. That is, until the New York City decorators discovered what was going on, and then the prices shot through the roof. But I got some nice pieces."

The tea was brewing as they talked, and he put out some biscuits that Francie had packed with the tea. He carried a tray with the tea and biscuits, napkins and mugs - no one took sugar or cream - to the living room. The tea was poured, the biscuits passed around, and

Ariane got down to business.

"Your house was very well built. Surprisingly so for the time, which I think was about sixty years ago. Very solid. The solidity means a little more work to drill through thicker walls, but also better security because we can set the sensitivity level to very high and you still won't get many false alarms."

Francie picked up the analysis. "We've decided to lay out the system tonight and come back in the morning to do the installation. It will be on and working, just not positioned where the heads will be when we install them. They will be less conspicuous."

Cody knew better than to ask if all this was necessary. He had seen the boxes of equipment and recognized most of the labels; the hardware only top professionals used. He wondered briefly about the price but knew that it was worth it.

When Francie and Ariane had finished their tea, they excused themselves and left to get the alarm sensors in place. Deki rose as they did to say good-bye. Cody walked him to the door. "If I haven't made it abundantly clear, Deki-san, I am most grateful for your good attention."

Deki bowed his head deeply and then looked back up at Cody. "I think at first you were worried that I might be a too frequent visitor," he said, and held up his hand when Cody began to protest. "This is more important than being neighbors, as you shall soon see. You must be in the moment, Cody-san, and never waiver." With that he turned and left Cody very much awake, and now significantly more alert.

XX

Francie and Ariane arrived at eight the next morning, carrying coffee and pastries. "Never show up empty-handed," Francie explained to Cody as she walked past him at the door and headed to the kitchen. "Oh, good. I'm glad to see that you cleaned up after last night. Even though it was late. Too many people, especially guys, leave the dishes until morning, and then leave them until the next morning."

"I'm glad I passed your test," he responded with a respectful smile.

She looked at him seriously and said softly, "We wouldn't be here if you hadn't passed the important tests, Cody. We want you to stick around."

Her tone brought him up short. "I appreciate that, Francie. And Ariane," he turned to face her. "And I want to stick around in large measure because of who you are, and the fact that you're here."

"*Bien sûr, mon ami*. And we have much work to do together. I don't know what this is with you," Ariane said, raising her eyebrows, "but certainly it is *très important*."

"Yes, exactly," Francie agreed. She nodded toward the pastries. "Now, we've been nibbling and sipping in the car and some of that you should save for us, but while we are doing the installation, enjoy. They are from Il Fornaio. Very good."

"*Merci bien, ma chere amie*," he told her.

"*O marveilleuse*. Another Francophile," said Ariane to Francie. "You chose well again." She closed with a broad smile in Cody's direction. "*Alors*, we have work to do."

"Right," her friend said with a nod, and off they went, discussing their approach to the installation as they headed for the stairs.

Cody sat at the dining room table, enjoying bites of different pastries and drinking his coffee as he perused a half-dozen websites on his laptop for the national and foreign news. He'd read into the local sources before breakfast had arrived. He added notes to a yellow legal pad about the stories he thought were important and others that might develop by five o'clock. From upstairs, and around the main floor and out in the garage, he heard the sounds of his security team, as he jokingly thought of them, at work. There was conversation, drilling, hammering, grunting, and there were various alarm sounds at different volumes.

It took only an hour because both were working, and when they returned to the living room, they reported that everything was working properly. "We need from you," Ariane said, "a four-digit code to set and deactivate the alarm. And also a five-digit code that will send an urgent emergency message to 911."

"Cody," Francie clarified, "We didn't know whether you wanted to contact the Carmel PD or the sheriff's office instead of 911. We think 911 would be better because you never know who's working where at what hours, if you get my drift."

"That's fine. I mean, unless I can't ring you two, or Bogie directly."

The women exchanged glances. Ariane said, "We thought about that. Would you prefer that?"

"Oh, goodness, I was joking...I thought."

There was a pregnant pause. "I know you, Francie, and expect that Ariane will be a friend, too. I would be most pleased to have you at the other end of the line, but I'm hesitant to put an added burden on you."

"*Ni plus ni moins*," Ariane said with a shrug. "It will not be a burden."

"She's right, Cody. If you need us, we'll be here, and with the right law enforcement. Besides, I don't think this will wind up being long term."

Cody nodded, "No, it shouldn't be."

"When are you going to air your Soledad story?" Francie asked.

"Not for a few weeks yet."

"*Non, mais oui.* But you are going to be investigating, yes?" Ariane confirmed.

Francie laughed and explained, "Ariane's beau was an anchorman in Sacramento. She knows the drill."

"Quite a group we are," Cody replied. "I look forward to meeting your beau."

"*Vraiment,* and he you. He knew of your work in Afghanistan."

Cody shook his head. "It's surprising to meet people who actually saw my reporting."

"If the Nielsen ratings are right, millions did, Cody."

Cody laughed. "I suppose so. I just didn't meet many of them before."

"*Bien,* so four digit to set and disarm?"

"How about two-six-three-nine?"

"*Mais non,*" Ariane responded immediately. "The first thing someone would guess is your name."

"How did you know that so quickly?"

"She thinks numerically," Francie said with a chuckle. "Besides, names are the most obvious, especially when they are four letters."

"How about seven-eight-two-six? My uncle's name was Stan."

"That's fine. And the five digit?"

"Two-three-three-five-three. My aunt Adele."

"*D'accord,*" Ariane acknowledged and with Francie stepped over to the keypad by the front door, where they keyed in the information. In a minute they were back. "You are all set. Try out the entry and exit code, but not the emergency. I tested that with my phone and it is working."

"I am so grateful to you both. I know this level of security is a good idea, especially since I'm working late. And I feel even better connected to you."

"We are ten minutes away," Francie told him. "Don't hesitate to call if you're simply not sure. No what-if's, please."

He watched them walk down to Francie's car. She opened the trunk and pulled out a small lawn sign which read Intercept Security Systems. She brought it back up his walkway and pushed it into the lawn. "These signs actually work. Even fake ones deter most burglars." She patted the top of the sign, waved good-bye, and walked back to her car.

Not long after they left, Cody got his things together and left the house. Then he walked back in and set the alarm, smiling to himself about the way he tracked things in his life, and sometimes didn't. All that rush installation of the system, and he had walked out the door without setting the alarm. He would have to, as he told Deki-san, be more in the moment.

Part of being more alert was checking the video feeds from his house. They had installed six tiny cameras that provided a fairly comprehensive look in and around the house. He could even get a panning shot of the street in front. Cody could see the output on his laptop, and even on his phone. In his first couple of hours at his office, he checked the cameras several times, mostly for amusement and to familiarize himself with what images the cameras provide. He saw nothing out of the ordinary.

He needed to focus most of his attention on the day's events to prepare for the early newscast, but he also had time to make calls to set up appointments to talk to people about the situation at Soledad prison. He was anticipating that he would produce two special reports for the news; one on the corruption of the guards and administration and the other on the gang leaders controlling their cartel operation from inside.

Cody scheduled his interviews for the mornings, before he needed to start prepping for the early newscasts. He'd made the decision to conduct the interviews one on one and privately, without a camera. He used a digital audio recorder for note-taking, but the sound wouldn't be used on the air. Even with audio distorted, some people were afraid, that they could be identified, and with what they had to say, that could put their lives in jeopardy.

Cody was fine with just quoting them when necessary. Even though this was television and he wouldn't have a wealth of video, the story would carry itself. The information was riveting, no matter how it was delivered And he certainly didn't want to be responsible for anyone getting hurt or even killed.

There was a certain degree of risk in even phoning some of the people he felt were important to his reporting, but they were at least as aware as he was of their own security. As a result, some people hung up on him as soon as he told them what he was working on. But using leads he'd gotten from the sheriff, Francie, and the two primary leads she had given him, Cody worked his way up the information food chain. He was not surprised at how far up he got.

And no, not everyone was camera shy. Cody easily arranged to tape an interview with the Deputy Director of Communications of the state Department of Corrections. Donna Mo even volunteered to come to Soledad prison to do the interview. It was set up for the warden's office the following week.

Then out of the blue – although as Deki-san had explained, there is no such thing as luck and nothing is ever out of the blue – Cody received a call from Slate Denidetto, a partner with the high-powered San Francisco law of Denidetto and Strauss. Actually, the call came from his executive assistant, who, when he got Cody on the line, put Denidetto on the line fairly promptly. Cody was familiar with the power games such people played and was pleased that he didn't have to wait.

Denidetto had learned through his own sources – ha, ha, ha – that Cody was planning a report on gang leaders running cartels from inside the prison. His client, Raphael Trujello, was a reputed leader of the *Mas Septo*, a Mexican cartel, who was doing life for ordering a dozen drug-related murders. "Of course he is innocent of those charges, you understand, Mr. Howard. He was set up to protect people in the cartel on the CIA payroll. It's very complicated, and I know that's not what your story is focused on but I thought you should know."

"I'd be glad to hear the details, Mr. Denidetto. May I infer that you would be willing to speak on camera, about your client's innocence and what role he might have in operating – or not – *Mas Septo*."

Denidetto laughed easily. "Well of course, Mr. Howard. I'd be glad to speak to both issues. But in fact, I was calling to see if you might be interested in speaking with Mr. Trujello himself. If I can arrange it. I'm not sure the prison officials will be willing, but I know Mr. Trujello would welcome the opportunity to speak with you on camera."

That part was a surprise and caught Cody aback for just a moment. "We would certainly welcome that opportunity, Mr. Denidetto. Let me ask, does Mr. Trujello speak English, not that that is essential, but for planning purposes, should the possibility come to pass?"

Another hearty laugh came down the line. "As well as you and me," the lawyer said. "Mr. Trujello graduated *magna cum laude* from UCLA."

"Did he?" Cody played along. "What was his major?"

"Political science with a minor in French literature. I'll have my executive assistant FedEx you an information package on this very interesting man when I am off this call with you."

"Thank you, Mr. Denidetto. And may I ask when you might expect to find out if this interview with your client might actually happen."

"I have a request into the Attorney General herself. I expect to hear in the next 24 hours."

"Very good. I'll look forward to hearing from you."

There was a click on the other end of the line. Cody was about to return the handset to the cradle but instead kept it to his ear. There was another, quieter click before the normal dial tone returned. "Hardly a surprise," he thought.

He sat mulling over the situation and then called Francie. She agreed to meet him after the early newscast. He didn't tell her why he wanted to talk to her, and she didn't ask. But when they sat down in a quiet corner of the empty living room at the Cypress Inn, she with a Bernardus Chardonnay and he with a Heller Cabernet, Cody outlined to her what he had been doing, whom he had called, and what were the results, including the second click on the phone line.

Francie received it all with a smile. "It's big time, isn't it? And I have to tell you, my friend, that what I'm hearing is good. The DofC and the cartel think they can play you."

"That was my impression," Cody acknowledged.

"And that suggests that no one is going to try to do you harm."

"As long as I don't threaten to do them harm."

Francie shook her head. "I don't think they are worried about you, Cody. They are too arrogant to think you can rock their boat. And as long as they think that, then it should be in their best interests to protect you."

"That's a kick in the pants, isn't it?"

"Better than a bullet in the head," Francie replied sternly. "No, I know what you're saying. Yes, you want results from your reporting on these two corrupt situations, side by side, and I sure there will be. Your job is not to fix them but to drag them out into the open. You bring out the facts, you get denials from the perps, and it's up to the pols to do something about it. Will they? The legislature may hold some hearings, but they get so little done as it is, I don't see them taking it very far. And anyway, you're out of it by then."

"I get the sense from what you're saying, and also from my conversations with the people at DofC and Trujello's attorney that they wouldn't be out to punish me, regardless of what happens."

Francie nodded. "It's funny, but yeah. It's kinda like professional courtesy." She laughed and raised her glass to him. He did likewise and they drank, to professional courtesy. She continued, "I knew a guy, Dave somebody, who was a reporter at WPRI in Providence. Rhode Island has a very influential, shall we say, organized crime presence. Dave was a good reporter, and sometimes he nibbled around the edges of their operation, but he never got in so deep that he was a threat to them.

"One day he was covering the funeral of a wise guy who had broken the rules. He was finishing up his standupper at the cemetery when three goons, looking really mean, started walking toward him. At that moment, a limo pulled up by the side of the road about fifty feet away. The goons froze. The back window came down. Dave could see the face of one of the mafia bosses.

"'Dave,' he said. 'Dave, come over here.' Dave walked over to the limo. 'Dave, I just wanna say, you know, I think you do a good job at what you do. You don't play nice, but you don't, you know, go dirty. I like that.' Then the guy reaches his hand out the window, snaps his fingers, and gestures for the goons to go away. Then he says, 'You be good, huh?' Then the window goes up and the limo drives off."

"Honor among thieves, or something."

"Or something. Dave was a good reporter. He wasn't scared off. He did his job. Covered the organized crime hearings, tapped into some snitches once in a while. But the Rhode Island mobs were tight. Anyway, I think that's the situation you've got here. I'm still glad you're packing...you are, aren't you?"

Cody might have reached for his pocket but instead he just gave her a short nod.

"And your house should be pretty safe or you should know it. Have you been checking the cameras?"

"Yes. Nothing unusual. Maybe a car parked across the street, but nothing worse."

"I think after your talk with Denidetto you shouldn't have any problems."

XXI

Cody had long given up the notion that coincidence was an adequate explanation for the concurrence of significant events. So when in a matter of a few hours, interviews with Donna Mo and Raphael Trujello at Soledad Prison were confirmed for the same day and an hour apart, the journalist had to laugh. He left his cubicle and told Belotti what happened. The assignment editor frowned.

"Do you think they're setting you up?"

"I think they think they are setting me up. The DofC is showing their willingness to cooperate, and Trujello wants to plead his case that he is innocent."

"That should be a story in itself. An exclusive."

"Yes, well, it will be part of a story. I'll wrap around whatever I've gotten from other sources and see how happy they are. It won't just be a he-said/she-said, not from what I've heard."

"You're not concerned that they might be very not happy?"

Cody looked at the man. "Yes, I'm concerned. I certainly don't want to make myself a target of either, but this is a legitimate news story, and it's an important one. If something happened to me, I'd expect consequences, and they'd know that as well. If just for political purposes, they'd be slapped down. They would have to decide if it would be worse just from our reports or if they took out their anger on a reporter. I suspect that they would be smart enough to realize that the former would be easier to take than the latter. Don't you?"

"For your sake, Cody, I hope so."

"Thanks, Nick. Can I have Felice for this shoot?"

"Sure. I'll tell her."

And so, two mornings later, Cody and Felice were plying the same route they'd taken on his first day, when it was supposed to be baptism by fire. It was six weeks later, and this time they weren't going to be denied entrance. They passed through the main and at the press gate, Lieutenant Reed's assistant gave them their credentials and waved them through. Through the open door, they could see Reed at his desk, not bothering to look up.

"Poor sport," Cody said after they had driven out of earshot.

Felice laughed. "And just for two set-up interviews. He should have been cheering us in."

They pulled into a visitor's space by the warden's office. Cody carried the lighting case and audio bag while Felice took her camera and tripod. They were shown to an empty conference room where she would set up the camera and a pair of lights while Cody was brought back to the warden's office to meet the man whose name was on the door and to connect with Donna Mo.

Deiter Pinthrift was former military; old military as in the first Gulf War. A large man who hadn't exercised much since driving across Kuwait, he sat some distance behind his desk because his stomach wouldn't let him get any closer. He wore a suit that was too small and mirrored sunglasses that were too large. Standing in front of his desk was Donna Mo, a tall, strikingly powerful-looking woman of probably black and Filipino roots who might have played professional basketball. She was wearing a bright green suit that was definitely not her color and hadn't been fashionable since Hillary Clinton had been in the White House.

Also in the room was a swarthy man in a Brioni suit and price tag-matching tie, shoes, and wristwatch. He also had three-points of a tie-matching handkerchief sticking out of the breast pocket of his jacket. Of course he was Slate Denidetto, Raphael Trujello's attorney.

There were handshakes and the usual palaver of insincere greeting, with Cody perfunctorily thanking them all for their cooperation, and promising that they would be ready to shoot Ms. Mo in about five minutes. Then he returned to the conference room.

"I don't find it terribly comfortable here, do you?" he asked Felice in a quiet voice.

Felice looked up from under her eyebrows, and without speaking, gave him his answer in deafening tones. She looked up at a clock on the walk – it read 10:30 – "If we're out of here before noon, I'll buy you lunch."

Cody nodded. "Let's try to do that. And Felice, if at any time you need to confer with me, just interrupt and say you have a technical problem that will take a few minutes to fix. Unmike whoever it is, and I'll say we'll call 'em back when it's fixed."

"Yeah, okay." She snapped her fingers several times to check the audio going into the camera and said, "Good to go."

Cody went back to the warden's office for the Department of Corrections official. When the others sought to follow, Cody held up his hand. "This is a private interview. I'm sure that Ms. Mo knows how to handle herself." There were glances all around but no protests. Cody brought her into the conference room, introducing her to Felice as he directed her to her seat. Felice miked her, and after a quick level check with the lights turned on, the interview began.

"Ms. Mo, we have received numerous reports that the management of this prison is corrupt, that officers are paid to ignore criminal activity, that the staff smuggles contraband into the prisoners including guns and drugs, and materials out for them, including directives for the operation of drug gangs on the outside, and that the prison management – indeed the Department of Corrections in Sacramento, is aware of this activity."

"My goodness, Mr. Howard, those are some allegations, and let me say that I will be glad to address them. But first I'd like to thank you for giving us the opportunity to tell our side of these allegations. I know you're a serious journalist, your work in Afghanistan should have earned you an Emmy, but so many reporters these days are just interested in the headlines, not the truth. So thank you."

And there she stopped. Cody waited a moment. "And regarding those allegations?"

"Oh yes, of course. Well you must know from your years as a journalist that especially when it is a matter of law and order, there are always people who don't like to be on the wrong side of the dock, so to speak, and they will try to stir up trouble to get a better deal. But Mr. Howard, these people are in prison because they broke the law, and particularly they are here at Soledad because they committed serious felonies. This is not a country club. They're here to do their time, not to have fun."

"And?"

She looked surprised. "And so they make up these stories to undermine the public's faith in the Department of Corrections. As they obviously are trying to do by spreading lies about what actually goes on here. Mr. Howard, please, you've met the warden, Colonel Pinthrift. Colonel Pinthrift has an impressive record of service in the military, fighting against Saddam Hussein, and in the past twenty years working for the people of California in maintaining order in our prisons, first at Corcoran and now here at Soledad. We are very gratified that he came to work with us."

"Ms. Mo, the majority of sources for the charges that I'm raising with you weren't prisoners. A few were former prisoners, but the rest were current and former guards, staffers, department officials, and attorneys."

"Oh," she said without showing any surprise. "Well, we will certainly look into this. I trust that you will share with us their names and contact information."

"No I won't. Considering the nature of the charges, revealing their identities to your department could put them at jeopardy."

"I must say I'm disappointed, Mr. Howard. I know that you are a reporter and want to have an exclusive, but how do you expect us to address your serious allegations – and let me say for the record that I take them only to be allegations, certainly not proven – if you won't even tell us the specifics of what you've been told. I'm sure your viewers would agree with me that you owe it to the people of California to provide the information you have so that we can investigate."

"Ms. Mo, are you suggesting that you were unaware of these charges?"

"Why certainly I was," she responded huffily. "I still am, since you won't tell me what you're talking about."

"Let me ask this, in the last four years that you've been Deputy Director of Communications, have you never had a discussion about these charges with others at the Department of Corrections?"

"No, absolutely not."

"You haven't written or read memos about allegations of impropriety at any of the state prisons."

She hesitated as critical suspicions kicked in but it was too late. Gamely she replied with a snort, "I have not. That would be a violation of the people's trust."

"Yes, to be clear, this is the first time you've heard any such charges or suggestions of impropriety by any of the department's officials, guards, or staff?"

"Yes."

"Uh, Ms. Mo, I don't mean it to seem as though I'm surprised at your answer, but you seem upset that I would even raise the issue. Corruption in prisons is not unheard of. There have been investigations and prosecutions of such activity in prisons around the country. And from what I've read, prisons in the United States aren't nearly as corrupt as many other places in the world. Yes?"

"Mr. Howard, I can't speak to the problems in other countries, I can only tell you that in California, we are proud of our management team and the people they have working under them to keep our prisons safe and secure. Yes, I am upset that these malicious innuendos are even being repeated, and by our own member of the California media."

Cody took a breath, and in a cheery-ish voice said, "That's all I have Ms. Mo. Do you have anything else that you'd like to put on the record?"

The fear in her eyes glinted briefly, along with hatred. "I've said all I need to, Mr. Howard." And with that she took off her microphone, got up, and walked out of the room without another word, closing the door behind her.

"Well that went well, I thought," Cody said, shaking his head.

Felice checked her recording. "We're good," she reported. "And here's the mini-DV copy I made for you as back up." She handed him the disk in a tiny sleeve.

He slipped it into an inner pocket, next to where he would have carried the Colt. He would have felt much more comfortable coming to the prison with the gun, but knew that if things went wrong, the pistol wasn't going to make a difference. And if they had searched him, and found him with an unregistered gun, his problems would have multiplied in a most discouraging direction.

The door opened, and in walked Raphael Trujello. Cody recognized him from his research. A squat man with a neat mustache, high forehead, and black eyes. He was fully shackled. His wrists were connected with just three links to a heavy chain around his waist. His ankles were also shackled closely together, with another chain running up to his waist. He was accompanied by a guard and his attorney. Cody knew there was no use – or sense – in asking that the interview be private. Nor did he relish the idea of being in the room with him without protection. And with the guard there, it made little difference if the attorney was too.

Cody stood but made no attempt to shake any hands. He merely pointed at the chair. Felice walked up to him and attached the microphone. Cody watched the prisoner as he stared at Felice, first her form as she approached and then her face, trying to force her to look at him. She acted with great calm and never looked up at him. She turned and returned to the camera, flicked a switch and instructed him to speak.

"*Buen cuerpa*," he said, leering at her.

"Sounds good," Felice said to Cody.

"Mr. Trujello, thank you for agreeing to do this interview."

"I'm always happy to talk with a member of the Fourth Estate, Mr. Howard. Especially someone such as yourself, a man of such significant repute."

"Sir, for years there have been stories about criminal enterprises being run by people from inside the nation's prisons."

"Yes, Mr. Howard, I have been aware of such reports."

"From your experience, would you say those reports are true?"

"Certainly they are."

His attorney coughed.

"Let me rephrase that for accuracy. I know that some reports are true, but I would have to know what specific reports you are referring to before I could confirm or deny them or simply tell you that I do not know the facts of that situation."

"What about here at Soledad prison? Are you aware of criminal enterprises being run by people here?"

"Is that one of the reports you might be referring to, Mr. Howard?"

"I have been told that you control a drug cartel known as *Mas Septo*. That it is based in Mexico but that its operations in the United States are divided and that you manage their activities west of Texas."

"That is not true, Mr. Howard."

"The specifics of what I described, or are you saying that you have no relationship whatsoever with *Mas Septo*, or any other organization involved in illicit activities?"

Trujello looked hard at the journalist and at the same time smiled. "Did you go to law school? You sound like you're taking my deposition?"

Cody chuckled. "No law school. I'm just trying to get clear answers. How about if I ask the questions separately?"

"No, it won't do any good. The answers are going to be the same. No. No. Or I should say yes and yes, I am saying I have 'no relationship whatsoever with *Mas Septo*, or any other organization involved in illicit activities.'"

"Where do you suppose these allegations come from, Mr. Trujello?"

"Oh, I don't know. How do they say it to the *New York Times*? 'Disgruntled former employees.'"

Cody saw the attorney shift in his chair.

"And what enterprise did you manage that these people might have been 'disgruntled former employees'?"

Trujello raised his eyebrows in respect. "Very good, Mr. Howard, very good." He took a deep breath and let it out. "I really couldn't say because I don't know who were these unhappy people."

"What have been the enterprises you've managed that had employees?"

Trujello's smile was gone. He turned to his attorney. "Didn't you give this man my resume? The one that lists my past business enterprises?"

"I thought I did, Mr. Trujello, but I'll make sure that he receives another copy when this interview is finished."

Trujello nodded once at the attorney and then looked back at the reporter. "Mostly I was involved in agriculture. Corn and tomatoes. We sold a lot of produce at farmer's markets and by the side of the road. That's how I got in trouble with the law. My employees, they didn't keep all the receipts."

"You are six years now into a life sentence for the killing of four people."

"To be clear, Mr. Howard, I wasn't accused of killing anyone. No one. I didn't kill anyone."

"You were charged and convicted of having ordered the killings of those four people. Why were those people killed?"

"Ah, you're being smart again." He said to the attorney. "This is a bright guy. We should have him in our enterprise...if we had one." He laughed. "I did not order anyone killed. I didn't kill anyone. I didn't even want anyone killed."

"Who were the four men in relation to you?"

"They were middle-level managers, as I recall. You know this case goes back maybe twelve years. The prosecutor gave deals to the actual killers. He told them if they testified I ordered them to do those killings, he wouldn't seek the death penalty." Trujello cocked his head back and looked at Cody for a long moment.

"You've been around long enough, Mr. Howard, to know how prosecutors work. They coerce the lower level people to take down the big guys. They threaten them or promise them something and they bite."

"And you were the big guy? The killers were your employees?"

Trujello sat up quickly, rattling his chains. His tone sharpened noticeably. "There you go again. The killers, the ones who did the killing and didn't get executed because they did what the prosecutors told them to do and ratted me out, yeah, they worked for the company, but that didn't mean I could order them to kill people." He sneered, "Any more than you could tell this cute number – hey, you and your friends – go kill someone and she would."

"Mr. Trujello, on another track, you are obviously well read. You are aware of current events. Is that fair to say?"

"Yeah," he replied, his voice redolent with suspicion.

"And I'm sure in preparation for your trial, you became knowledgeable about the drug trade and the Mexican cartels?"

"So?"

"What effect do you think decriminalization of drugs would have on the cartels?"

Trujello's eyebrows rose. "You're asking me like I'm one of those experts on Fox News?"

"You must know more about the subject than most of those so-called 'experts' I would expect."

Trujello looked over at his attorney and then back at Cody. He looked long and hard at the reporter before saying, "I guess I probably do know more. Yeah, I did a lot of research for my trial." He quickly looked over at his attorney then back again. "It didn't do me much good, as you can see. But what's your point?"

"I just wondered what you thought would happen to the drug cartels if drugs were legalized. If buying drugs – marijuana, cocaine, heroin – wasn't illegal, would the prices drop so much as to take the profit out of it?"

"I don't know, maybe. It's nothing I really know about. It doesn't affect me."

"What does affect you, Mr. Trujello?"

"What do you mean, what affects me?"

"You are here in Soledad with virtually no chance of being pardoned or paroled, what do you think about?"

Trujello scowled at the journalist. "First you're a prosecutor, now you're a shrink. What's up with you? I'm done." He gave Cody a hostile look. He started to walk away and realized he was still wired. He leered at Felice. "*Hola, cariño,* come close to Raphael."

Felice looked to Cody. "Are we done?"

"Apparently," he replied.

"'Apparently' you say. You don't know."

"Why are you so angry with me, Mr. Trujello?" Cody demanded in a stern but even voice. "What else did you expect me to ask you? I would think someone as smart as you would appreciate a good interview."

The tone caught the prisoner and Trujello stopped to digest what he'd just heard. He knew it was true but to acknowledge it would be to lose control. In the few seconds that he was distracted by Cody, Felice stepped over and removed the microphone from his jumpsuit. By the time Trujello looked at her again, she had stepped out of reach of whatever he thought he might do or say and had turned away from him.

Trujello stopped in front of Cody who had stood up when the prisoner had. "You know, I could have been mad at you, but you're right. You did ask the fair questions. Maybe sometime we can do this again."

Cody nodded his head. "Good. I know you have a lot to say."

Trujello looked him hard in the face one last time and then headed for the door. The attorney opened it for him and then followed him out, the guard leaving last.

"We're wrapped," Cody said to Felice. He looked up at the clock. It was 11:40. "You owe me lunch."

Felice was already coiling cable. "In Monterey. Maybe by then I'll get my stomach back."

Cody nodded. "Yes, me too. I'll be right back to help with the gear. I have to say my good-byes."

He went into the hall and down a couple of doors to the warden's office. Without knocking he opened the door. All the players were standing around the warden's desk and looked up at him in surprise. "Warden, I just wanted to say thank you for making this possible. I know it wasn't fun for anyone. But I do appreciate the effort you and your people, and Ms. Mo and Mr. Trujello made under the circumstances." Then he withdrew, closing the door behind him.

He walked back to the conference room and in three minutes, the lights had been broken down and stowed in their cases, the cables were rolled up, and the tripod lowered. Cody picked up the lights and tripod and suggested, "I'm hungry. Let get out of here."

"Follow me," Felice said, and they were driving toward the gate a minute later. But just as they were approaching the PIO building, they saw Lieutenant Reed rush out the door and wave them down.

"Oh shit," Felice said, earning a startled look from Cody. "Sorry."

"No need to apologize," he said as she slowed down the car. "I would have said it if you hadn't."

She pulled up to a stop and Reed walked around to Cody's window. "The warden said to give you this." He handed him a DVD. "It's shots from inside and outside this place that he had taken because you would have caused disruptions and not gotten the cooperation he did. He said you would probably want it for your report."

"Thanks, Lieutenant. Please thank the warden for us."

"Will do." With that he backed off and Felice drove off toward the main gate. It wasn't until they were through and then turning onto Highway 101 that they both let out an audible sigh of relief."

"This reminds me," Cody said, "of flying out of Moscow before the government fell. People on the plane were very quiet until the pilot announced that we were out of Soviet airspace and then there was applause and laughter."

XXII

Felice was ready to buy lunch but Cody insisted, telling the waitress at The Green Tee to give him the bill. It had been an interesting lunch as they played back the events of the morning. From the two interviews to the scare when they saw Lieutenant Reed flagging them down.

"Did you, even for an instant, think of running him down?" Cody asked her.

"Longer than an instant," she replied with a laugh. "I have never wanted to get out of some place more in my life. Well, that's not quite true. I was once in a building that caught fire and the place was filling with smoke, but at least then I knew what was going on."

"What was your take on Trujello?"

"I was very concerned when he threatened you at the end, but the way you handled him was really smart." She nodded at him. "You probably saved your life."

"It was that close, wasn't it?" A smile broke out on his face. "You handled him well. What did he say to you? If I might ask."

"Oh, he said I had a nice body."

"That's not awful, I mean, what he could have said."

She looked at him. "I've heard a lot worse. I've miked a lot worse. But you know, he gets, um, women in there."

"I've heard that there is little that the prison walls keep out, for the inmates with clout and money."

"Sex, drugs, booze, and big screen TVs, they got it all."

"I wonder if that doesn't reduce the rate of violence inside."

"Maybe it does. Nothing is simple these days, is it?"

"Seems not."

After lunch they drove back to the station. They watched the video that had been shot at the prison by the warden's people. It was professionally done and would help to flesh out the reports. Then Felice made back-up copies of what she had shot, and Cody went up to Burgess' office to tell him what they'd gotten at the prison.

The news director showed remarkably little interest in what he had to say. "So what are you thinking of doing with it? When are you going to have scripts for me to look at?"

Cody didn't show his displeasure. "I'm now thinking of three reports running two-minutes-thirty each for the Tuesday, Wednesday, and Thursday of the first week in the next sweeps period. That's a few weeks away, the beginning of August, right?"

Burgess grunted.

"I'm going to screen all the video, and I have a couple more off-camera interviews to do, so I should have scripts to you next week. How's that?"

Burgess grunted again. "We don't have any money in the budget to promote the thing, you know?"

"I wasn't counting on it, Herb. But when I have it all cut, I'll ask you to show it to Big Don, and maybe he'll find some funds for promotion. Or maybe an advertiser will want to sponsor it."

"I doubt it."

Cody shrugged. "You know better," he said as he stood to leave. When Burgess remained silent, Cody left his office and waited until he'd turned the corner to let his feelings show on his face. As he took the stairs back down to the main level, he reconsidered the efforts he had made to avoid stepping on his toes. He had studiously avoided confrontations with the man by checking first with him on issues that might possibly be construed as poaching on his territory. It hadn't seemed to make a difference. If the reports on the prison turned out well, he would take the matter to the station manager. While Cody didn't want Burgess' job, his own job would be a lot easier if he had the clear authority to do the news as he thought it should be done.

When he got to his desk there were two messages, one from Felice saying the recordings they'd done that morning were good, and the other from Francie, suggesting they meet at his house for a cuppa after his early newscast, and to call her only if that wouldn't be possible. Immediately on alert, he went online to check the cameras at his house. In one shot he saw that there was a carton sitting in front of the front door. He assumed that Francie had seen the carton and wanted to make sure that he dealt with it properly.

He couldn't remember having ordered anything but that didn't mean that something hadn't been sent to him; something that he actually wanted. It was farfetched, he told himself, to think that someone had left a bomb or some other kind of destructive device on his doorstep. With some effort, he put the thought out of his mind and working on his early newscast.

At 5:45 he pulled up in his car across the street from his house, just behind Francie's car, and as he did so, both she and Ariane got out.

"I saw that you checked out the cameras after you got my note."

"You can tell when I do that?" he asked. "I didn't know that. Whatever has happened to privacy in our country?"

"For better or ill, there really is none."

"That's what I was feeling," Cody admitted. "And you didn't like the idea of the box on my doorstep?"

"Your neighbor," Francie said, giving a nod toward Deki's house, "said an individual, not a delivery service, had left it."

"How was he carrying it?"

Francie gave him an approving look. "Not like it was fragile or about to explode."

"*Mon ami*, are you expecting any deliveries?"

"Not that I can think of Ariane, but sometimes I order something and it takes a while to arrive. Anyway, that would most likely arrive by UPS or FedEx. Isn't that what we were thinking? Why you are here?"

"*Cher* Cody, if you ever decide you don't like the news business, you maybe can partner up with Francie and become a consulting deputy."

Cody laughed. "I'll keep that in my back pocket," he said. "Now what do we do about the box. It's on my doorstep. Is there any reason why I shouldn't just go look at it?"

Francie and Ariane exchanged glances. "I think that should be all right," Francie said. "But don't move it or shake it. See if it has a label on it."

"I can do that," he said, and he walked across the street and up his walkway. When he got to the doorstep, he stopped and craned his neck, peering at the top of the box. He turned back to them with a smile. Then he walked back to the where they were waiting by the cars. "It's a box from L. L. Bean and it's addressed to me at the wrong address. It says South Palm Drive instead of North Palm. Someone crossed out 'South' and wrote in 'North' and 'delivered to wrong address'."

Francie and Ariane looked at each other thoughtfully. "And had you ordered from them recently?"

"No," he said, "but it's not impossible that my parents sent me something. They do that sort of thing. And they love L. L. Bean."

The three exchanged glances. "I'm not sure how paranoid I should be, but I will defer to your professional judgement. With respect and appreciation, I should add."

"Silver-tongued anchor," Francie said to Ariane with a straight face.

"*Oui, c'est vrai.* I know it well since I have one of my own at home."

Francie laughed. "So what do you think? Do we need to call Mike?"

"Better him than the locals. If you think we should?"

"Who's Mike?" Cody wanted to know.

"Mike Olsen. FBI in Salinas. Good guy."

"How about I take a ride over to South Palm and ask the person if he brought over the box?"

"*Bon idée.* Francie, you should have thought of that. Should one of us go with him?"

"Do you know who lives at that address?" Francie asked.

Cody shook his head.

"Or how he should know that you live at this address?"

He shook his head again, but more slowly this time.

"And it hasn't happened before?"

"Not since I've been here."

France frowned. "I'll go over with you and stay in the car."

She and Cody got into his car and drove the six blocks from North to South. There was a number "308" there, and Cody walked up to the house and rang the bell. The door was answered by a man who had a brief conversation with him. They were smiling when they shook hands, and Cody returned to the car.

"Nice fellow. He said for years there had been wrong deliveries. It had almost always gone to South Palm when it should have gone to North Palm. He said he thought maybe a half-dozen times in the past few years. I promised to bring him anything mis-delivered to my house."

"And you were satisfied that he was legitimate?"

Cody peered at her. "You think he might have been part of a conspiracy?

Francie shook his head. "That would be a stretch, but I asked in case there was something in the back of your mind that needed jogging. It happens sometimes your intuitive has an itch that needs scratching, that's all."

"I like that," he told her. "It kinda ties in with some of the things that Deki-san has been talking to me about. Interesting guy."

"Interesting indeed," Francie said. "You know that it was he who got you your house?"

"How's that?"

"He owned it and put it in a trust so you wouldn't know he was behind your move."

"Why would he do that?"

Francie shrugged. "Probably so you wouldn't think he was interfering in your life. To make sure you had a feeling of independence from your neighbor."

"But why did he want me to move in? He didn't know who I was before I moved in. As I told you, I hadn't even come to see the house before I bought it."

"He's a very interesting man, Cody. He sees things most people don't. He's more in touch with his own energy than anyone I've met. He's a fifth degree black belt in *aikido*. I saw him training once. He could throw people twice his size across the mat and have them land gently."

Cody whistled. "So why did he want me in his house? My house," he corrected.

"Because, my friend," she said, patting his leg, "he knew who you were, as a person."

Cody flashed a glance at her. "Francie, I didn't get any of this stuff when I was growing up. Did you?"

"Not from my parents, not directly. But I knew there was something larger about life than what had been explained to me. I didn't know what it was, but I sensed that there was a sub-text – or maybe a super-text – that they didn't know. Or maybe people knew it, but they weren't conscious of it. If that makes sense?"

Cody nodded. He pulled up behind her car. "When I talk with him, he speaks of things that I knew but hadn't been aware of."

Francie nodded. "That's the stuff."

They got out of the car and joined Ariane. As Francie related their news, Cody walked up to the house. He took out the small pocketknife he had on his key ring and carefully slit the tape sealing the top of the box. He stepped back and gingerly pulled back one of the flaps. Then the others. He looked in the box, and carefully moved around what he saw inside. He took out a packing slip and read it.

"Two chamois shirts and a belt, from my parents," he said to the two friends standing by the car. "I'm going to bring it inside, and then we can get something to eat?"

Francie showed him a thumbs up, and twenty minutes later they were sitting in a booth at Baja Cantina.

"How is it that you developed your intuitive? Did you do meditation or have teachers?"

"*Mais oui*, you can do both. Or you can have something happen and say, 'What the hell is going on here?' and then listen very carefully for an answer."

Cody was ready to laugh but he saw that the woman was serious.

"I learned a lot on the *aikido* mat," Francie told him, "pushing my thoughts away and trusting my instincts to act. The more I did it, the faster it happened, and it came from deeper inside of me."

"*Moi aussi*. That's where I met Francie, when Geoffrey and I first moved here from Sacramento. On the *aikido* mat. She knew the *aikido* better because I hadn't been training; my father had been sick. That wasn't the right excuse, but that's what I had told myself. *Peu importe*. I had been doing a lot of meditating and listening to music. It helped me get to new places inside."

Francie reached over and brushed her friend's cheek with her finger tips. "I knew the first time I saw her that she was my sister."

Ariane smiled and then laughed. "You remember how that man...?"

Francie laughed. "*Bien sûr, chere amie.* It was Ariane's first time on the mat at the Monterey *dojo* and, I don't remember the exercise it was, but it involved brushing one's hand up from the waist in front of the opponent to distract her. This *uke* – this man she was training with, brushed his hands across her chest."

Ariane picked up the story. "I was furious, but I was new there. But Francie saw what he did, as did our *sensei*. She signaled that we should do the same exercise with new partners. Francie came over to work with that man. And then instead of bringing him down softly to the mat, she threw him down hard. Very hard."

Francie chuckled and said to her, "I don't think he ever came back."

"If my Geoffrey had been there, he would have had some trouble walking."

The three laughed. Their food arrived, and knowing that Cody had to return to the station shortly, they dug in. But between bites, they shared some more of their experiences. Francie offered, "What it comes down to is what I think it was George Leonard – he was one of the early people at Esalen, a very good man – spoke of once. He had been training in his energy awareness, and had spoken of soft eyes. And then to one of the advanced groups he said, 'You can approach life with a soft mind. An open mind. One without the hard edges, the self-imposed limitations, or the useless thoughts.'"

"*C'est ça*, that was a very special moment. I remember," said Ariane, "he said that with soft mind, you only see what is important. You focus on what you need to see. It is effortless. In soft mind, you become one with the universe and in a way, you know everything. You are aware that you are connected to everything."

Cody was bringing a bite of his dinner to his mouth and stopped. "I wonder if that isn't like what athletes talk about. The quarterback, Joe Montana, saying that suddenly everything was in slow motion. He could throw perfectly to the receiver. Or Tiger Woods, who said the hole looked as big as a garbage can lid."

"*Mais oui*, I think it is the same thing." Ariane looked at Francie who nodded her head.

"Anyone can get into that space. They just have to know that it's there, and then how to drop – or is it rise? – into it."

"So," Cody asked, "What were your intuitive readings on the box on my doorstep?"

Francie laughed. "I thought it was safe, and I thought it was a worthwhile exercise to check it out."

"*Vraiment*. It is rare that you will get an absolute indication from your intuition over your cognitive mind. Very little is black and white. So it is important that you listen carefully for the quality of the indication. If it isn't a strong indication, you need to maybe back off a decision until you have more information."

"Agreed, and in this case, checking on the appearance of the box and then going over to meet your neighbor. Oh yes, sometimes you will have to act quickly, but when you have doubts, you should usually take your time and ask."

"Ask?"

"Open your mind more. Relax your thought process. Often you are under stress and it tightens your brain. It narrows your thinking and limits what you will consider. That is why soft mind is so important. It lets in more information."

Cody shook his head. "This seems so obvious, and so important. Why don't they teach this is school? Why didn't my parents tell me this?"

Francie patted his forearm and then briefly left her hand on it. "We come into the world with this knowledge, Cody, and it is taught out of us. It was necessary for social organization. The members of a society depended on each other for survival. Now we are in a time of transition where social structure will be transformed so that people will contribute from their intuitive instead of just their cognitive. And the intuitive will be fed by a far more advanced source – call it the universe, the force, or simply what created life – and we'll do away with much of the negativity."

"Now that will be a news story," said Cody. "Film at eleven."

XXIII

For the next two weeks, in addition to his regular newscasts, Cody worked on the special reports on the situation at Soledad prison. His first report was on the management of Soledad prison, the second on the cartel control on the inside and their reach outside, and the third on the prison situation nationally, He thought briefly about going over the head of his news director and showing the pieces to Big Don, but he relented to his better self and put them on the intranet for Burgess to see.

When Burgess had failed to even acknowledge them after two days, Cody went up to his office. "Did you see the special reports on the prison?" he asked without sitting down.

Burgess looking at him for a long moment before he answered. "Yeah, I saw 'em."

"Any comment?"

He shrugged. "Considering all the money we put into 'em, I guess we have to run them."

Cody had to restrain himself. In fact he was pleased with himself that he didn't let go at the man with what he might have said long ago. "Aha," was all Cody said, then he turned and walked down the hall to the station manager's office.

Big Don was sitting behind his desk, and he greeted his anchor with a pleased grin. "How's my star anchorman?"

"Good morning, Don. I've finished the special reports on Soledad. I'd like you take a look at them. They're on the intranet. Please let me know what you think of them."

"Glad to, Cody. Where are they?"

Cody gave him the code.

"Sit down," Big Don said, pointing to a chair, "if you've got the time."

Cody did. Big Don typed in the code. The spots ran in sequence. When they were done, the station manager turned to Cody and said, "Cody, I am so glad you came to Monterey. Those are some of the best pieces of journalism I've seen in a very, very long time. I'm more proud than I can say that they are going to run on KMTY. They are dynamite. How do we promote them?"

Cody was delighted. "Oh, I'm so pleased you feel that way." He left some innuendo in his voice to prompt the station manager's response. First there was silence and then he was asked, "Has Herb seen them yet?"

"Yes."

"And?"

Cody was done with office politics. "He said, 'Considering all the money we put into 'em, I guess we have to run them.'"

"Did he?" Big Don shook his head. "I thought this might be coming." He looked down at his hands folded on his desk. He raised his eyes up to Cody. "You must have too."

Cody didn't say anything but when Big Don's silence required an answer he said, "I didn't come here to anchor, but the way my work has been received by you and the community has given me a new lease on my career. I'm really pleased, as you can tell, about these reports and your response to them. Journalism, real journalism, has always been what I'm about."

The station manager nodded his head. "It's not about you." He took in a long breath and let it out softly. "All right. I'll talk to him first and then you and I can settle things. You can handle both jobs, I think. We'll figure that part out."

Cody stood up. He reached across the desk and shook Big Don's hand. Then he turned and went down to the newsroom.

His mind was spinning. It certainly wasn't unheard of for a news director and anchor to hold both titles, and in much larger markets. While he didn't have administrative or management experience per se, he did know how to get the best out of people who were on the same page when it came to quality news. He thought about how the mood had changed at KMTY since he'd become anchor not even three months earlier. There was a noticeably stronger commitment to news. The unforced errors had declined over that time. The tone of conversations among the staff had gotten more grown-up. The coordination between the shooters and the reporters was tightening up. There was a feeling that this was no longer just a jumping-off spot, a place to develop a new demo reel to show to consultants for a look in a larger market.

He would have to have true support. He wondered if Nick Belotti would be behind him. Relations between the two men had improved over the brief time they'd been thrown together, and Belotti hadn't been treated well by Burgess. He would have to see. Cody smiled. What he had tapped into with Deki-san, Francie, and Ariane suddenly seemed a prelude to this next step.

He shook his head as if to empty it of its myriad thoughts. He didn't know what might be the timetable for the change, and if he spent any time dwelling on it, it would distract him from his work. First his newscasts, and then how to get the best audience for the special reports. He knew the reach could be national as well as local and in Sacramento.

He decided that he should show it to Francie to get her take on it, both as a journalist and knowing the lay of the land locally. Also, to make sure that he was not putting himself into unwarranted danger. He had been very careful with the scripts, making sure that he reported the facts as he had gathered them, and he could in no way be perceived as prosecuting an agenda, either personal or in regards to the prison system.

As he reported in the first piece, America had more people behind bars per capita than all but a few countries, and the recidivism rate was around 75% five years after a prisoner was released. Obviously our criminal justice system wasn't working. It was a national issue, but his viewers – and those in the rest of the state – didn't have too look far to bring the problem home.

It wasn't his job to proscribe solutions, though he did include a sound cut from a prison reform expert in the final report. Her recommendations would be considered radical by many but they made sense. First was to decriminalize drug use, gambling, and prostitution; the so-called victimless crimes. That would dramatically reduce the prison population and free the police and courts to deal with violent criminals.

Her second suggestion was that we distinguish between violent and non-violent offenders, keeping the former locked up until they no longer threatened society, and putting the property criminals into work-release programs so that they could repay their victims and the community. She estimated that such reforms could generate between fifty and a hundred billion dollars a year in budget savings while making the country much safer.

He texted Francie to find out when she might be available. She responded immediately, asking if he wanted just to see her or with Ariane. He answered her in the singular.

"People are gonna talk." Francie wrote back.

Cody laughed and suddenly saw a light flash in a corner of his consciousness. Then he smiled. He typed back, "One of my favorite songs is Bonnie Raitt's 'Something to Talk About.' But my original thought was to ask you to look at the Soledad pieces."

"Glad to. When's good?

"Not urgent. You have time this weekend?"

"Sure. Come over for dinner tomorrow night? "

"Yum. What time? Red or white?"

"Six. Both. I'm at Yankee Point. Here are direx." She included a link to a Google map to her home.

Cody wrote, "Looking forward to it" and then thought about saying more before hitting the send button. He sent it as it was.

A short time later Francie texted him back. "Me too," it read.

"When it rains...." he thought.

XXIV

Cody was ready to lounge between the sheets, it being Saturday morning, but he awakened at the top of a sleep cycle and realized that it would be near-impossible to climb back into the arms of Morpheus. Instead he got up and turned on his computer. While his old PC booted up, he started some coffee. When he settled before the screen and checked his mail, his calendar popped up a reminder of an appointment he had completely forgotten. He smiled at the reasons that it had been pushed from his mind – the workplace situation and Francie.

The reminder that he was to be at the sheriff's recruits center that day to meet with Deputy Ursula DeVine. The sheriff had arranged for him to meet with one of his prized training officers to sharpen Cody's situational awareness skills. Or as the deputy explained them, "These are things you should know so that you can avoid being surprised by an attacker...and what you should know in the event of an attack."

As he told Francie later, the deputy was, if inadvertently, well-named. "She's my height, about six foot, and probably weighed about the same, too – most of it is muscle. She probably works out a couple of hours every day. Her physique is solid Amazon, but she is thoroughly feminine in the way she speaks and the way she carries herself. And to top her off, so to say, she is blond with blue eyes, and she's pretty."

The deputy was also all business, and what she had to teach complemented all of the police training Cody had had, and then took it a step further. Using a staged set and later videos, she showed him how to scan a room, identifying not only people but also potential threats; for instance, people who were looking at him too often – a more complicated situation for a public figure such as himself. Also, she reminded him something that he already knew but didn't put into effect enough; he needed to sit with his back to the wall whenever possible, and to be in a position to see the entrances and emergency exits.

She pointed out how difficult it was to pull a gun while sitting down, and to take note of possible weapons like knives and forks, hot coffee, flower vases, and furniture. She showed him how to use crowds to his advantage if he needed to leave quickly, and once out of a building, where to find safe sites outside.

"If someone is confronting you, it's important to remember the rule of twenty-one. Have you learned that yet?"

Cody scratched his head. "I seem to remember someone having mentioned it but not explaining it."

"Twenty-one is twenty-one feet. When someone is twenty-one feet away from you, you have a chance to act but only about a second. Even if you're pointing your gun at someone with a knife who is closer than that, you probably won't have the time to react if he comes at you.

"Distance is your best defense in a confrontation. Even if it's not about guns and knives. If someone is being threatening, you can hold your hands up in front of you to slow things down. Or if you have martial arts training, and you might try that because it's good for both your physical and mental health in addition to self-defense, going into a martial arts stance will almost always cause an attacker to think twice."

Then the deputy explained when to use a car to escape, and they took a ride in Cody's car across Highway Sixty-Eight to Salinas. As they were driving, the deputy demonstrated how to scan on the open road and in traffic; to pick up a tail and keep it or lose it.

Back at the training center, Ursula, for that's what he was calling her by the last phase of the training, showed him how to deal with close-in attacks. When he was held from behind, his best course might be to stomp on the attacker's foot as the metatarsal bones were particular vulnerable because they sat over the empty arch in the shoe.

She demonstrated how to use his elbows and the heel of his hands rather than his fists. She also noted how effective his ubiquitous Cross ballpoint pen could be for stabbing someone.

"The most important lesson, and you may have picked this up in your prior training," she said, "or from the troops when you were in Afghanistan, is that you never fight to lose."

Cody laughed. "I know where you are going with this. I worked with a cameraman from the Chicago bureau who used to spar verbally with one of the soundmen. John was maybe five-ten, and the sound guy six-two. When it got dicey once, John's voice got really hard and he told the soundman what he was going to do if the man was dumb enough to get physical with him, including gouging his eyes.

"The soundman looked horrified and objected, telling John that would be dirty fighting. And John said, 'If someone pushes me into a fight, I do what it takes to make sure he doesn't do it again.' And he told the kid, 'cause the guy was about fifteen years younger, that he didn't wait to see how the fight was going. He started dirty and ended it fast."

Ursula nodded her head at the wisdom. "Your friend got it right. You don't feel your way into a fight. You end it. There were countless stories throughout military history of smaller, unarmed men over-whelming stronger armed soldiers and guards." She shrugged. "It was more important to them to win."

"Ursula," Cody began as they were walking out to the parking lot at the end of the training, "someone was talking to me the other day about soft mind. Have you worked with that?"

They had just gotten to their cars. She stopped and smiled at the reporter. "I didn't know you'd had that kind of training."

"I haven't. Not formally." He explained to her in brief the substance of the conversations he'd had with Deki-san, Francie, and Ariane. A smile of appreciation bloomed on the deputy's face.

"Very good. I'm impressed that you responded so favorably to it."

"Why is that?"

She sighed, "Most of my trainees – remember, they're training to be cops – and especially those who are originally from the East Coast, they aren't so open to Eastern concepts. And while I don't train many – you may be the first – reporters, I'd think they would be skeptical of something that requires, well, a soft mind."

Cody laughed. "You're probably right."

"So how is it that you were receptive to it? Maybe it will help me with some of the people I work with."

Cody cocked his head. "I'll give it some more thought and get back to you, but just off the top of my head, I found it appealing because it makes sense. More input. Broader vision. Less sensory prejudice."

"Oh, I like that. Thank you." She reached out and shook his hand. "I really enjoyed working with you."

"This was good for me, too, Ursula. You're very good at what you do. I think it's because you listen rather than lecture. There is an old Buddhist, I think, saying that the best teacher knows herself to be a student."

'Yes, I'd heard that. It's what makes teaching so satisfying."

"Hey, have you ever thought of giving training to non-law enforcement? I would think much of what you teach would have applications beyond self-protection and into simply broader thinking."

"Soft mind?"

"Soft mind.

She laughed. "Funny you should ask. I've been thinking it may be time to break with the sheriff's office. Bogie – the sheriff – is great but there is a lot of union stuff that makes the job more difficult. I thought if I went on my own, I could be hired back as a consultant and not have to deal with the bureaucratic nonsense and the sniping. I could also deal with professionals some of the time, instead of over-amp'd guys who haven't grown up yet and who think police work is all about being macho."

"Keep me apprised, will you, Ursula? Maybe we could do a profile of you sometime."

Her face lit up. "Really? That would be so neat."

XXV

It was at precisely six o'clock when Cody knocked on Francie's front door. It was only a few seconds later when she opened the door, welcoming him with a warm smile.

"I so appreciate you being on time. Television news people must have a special gene in them." She stepped back and he walked into the spacious living area. He stopped to take it in. On the east wall was a modern kitchen with a long prep island with it's own sink and a grill, plus space for two settings with a view back through the kitchen windows, up to the coastal ridge on the far side of Highway One. On the open side of the island was an open corridor that led to the south wing of the house, and on the other side was the dining area, a table for eight set for two, and beyond that, two steps down was the living room. Most of the west wall was glass, windows and French doors. Beyond was a deck, with a hot tub on one side, and then a long area of natural grasses and gorse stretching some seventy-five feet to a sheer cliff that dropped another thirty feet to the rocks that edged the Pacific Ocean.

On the north and south walls were five-foot high shelves with a widely varied collection of art and bric-a-brac, and several more floor-to-ceiling shelves filled with a comfortable disorder of books of every sort. He looked forward to checking out the scope of her library another time. Above the shelves were a number of pieces of art, some old, some new. Again, the collection was indefinable.

"How lovely, Francie," Cody said, the vibrance in his voice underscoring how clearly impressed he was.

"Why thank you, Cody. Come along. Why don't you open the red..." There was an opener and glasses on the island. "...and I'll put the white in the fridge." She did so. "Would you like a quick tour?"

"Please," he said as he uncorked the red. "I hope it was all right not to get a regular white. I tried Caraccioli's Brut Cuvee the other night and found it very pleasant." He put the bottle in the refrigerator, his reporter's eyes quickly noting the content and order. "While I was there I picked up their Pinot Noir."

"I love champagne, even though we're not supposed to call it that."

"Why is that? How did the French get a lock on the name?"

"Funny you should ask. A friend of mine was doing some research for a screenplay she is writing and found out that Champagne was defined as being from the Champagne region in France where they'd been growing grapes since the first millennium and was producing the stuff according to an *appellation d'origine contrôlée*. This was set by an 1891 treaty and reaffirmed by the Treaty of Versailles at the end of the First World War."

Cody's eyes widened in bemusement.

Francie laughed. "Aren't you glad you asked?"

"I'm ready for Trivial Pursuit. Still, I'd be happy if other vineyards could call their champagne champagne, but maybe with a small c."

"Not in our lifetimes." She led Cody to the north wing of the house. A short hallway led to a fully-furnished spare bedroom with its own bathroom, a large storage room/pantry, and the garage. "I refer to that as the guest room but I never have guests. I don't have a lot of people I really want to visit from outside this area, and if they do come, I can find them a nice room at the Highlands Inn or the Cypress Inn in Carmel. I don't prefer my privacy, I need it. This is my sanctuary."

"I can understand that. And what a marvelous place to enjoy it. I've driven down to Big Sur a few times, but I never realized what was here. It's marvelous."

"It is," Francie agreed as she took his arm and walked him back through the main part of the house to the other wing. "And this is where I spend much of my time." Again there were three doors. One she opened into a large linen closet that also had a large custom-built wine cellar.

"I can see why you'd spend a lot of time in here," Cody joked.

She closed the door and entered a large room that might have originally been the master bedroom but which she used as an office. It contained two desks in an L-shape configuration, a couple of other work tables, covered in an orderly way with files, papers, and some electronic gear. The view from the main desk was across the back yard to the ocean. In the back wall, there were doors which Francie opened and then re-closed, to a walk-in closet and a bathroom.

"I think a lot of people, if they saw your set-up, would have to ask how you could get any work done, with such a view."

"Yes, they would. Maybe they aren't interested in what they are doing. But I, like you, love my work. I have no problem doing what needs to be done, and enjoying the view as a way to clear my head."

Cody laughed.

"What?"

"I was thinking of my cubicle at KMTY. Maybe I'll put up a couple of posters."

Francie looked into his face. "You mean now that it looks like you'll be staying?"

Cody didn't answer immediately. The question was significant, but he was suddenly noticing just how attractive was this woman. Not just physically, but in that moment, her eyes shone with a light that reached down to her soul.

"Yes," he said in a thoughtful tone that covered a lot of ground. "Yes," he repeated, "It looks like that."

Francie knew what the answer covered, and without breaking her gaze, she told him, "Good." Then she nodded her head toward the door. "C'mon. The tour's almost over and I think the Pinot's had enough time to breathe." She walked to the other side of the wing and into her bedroom.

"I took this smaller suite for my bedroom since I wasn't going to be in here much, except at night and didn't really need the view."

"Makes sense," Cody agreed as he admired the quiet class of the room. The queen bed against the north wall, a high window in the east and south walls that would provide the morning light. Unlike her office, which was painted and featured several prints on the wall, the walls in the bedroom had been papered in a flowered print of muted colors, and topped by ivory crown molding. There were two matching bedside tables and on the other side of the room were a bureau, and a lounge chair that matched the coverlet on the bed.

"No TV," Cody observed.

Francie smiled. "Not in my bedroom. It's bad enough, watching television before I go to sleep. And now with you on the air, I stay up every night to find out what's going on in my world and community. But I'll watch in my office. Or in the living room. There's a big screen for watching movies behind one of the tapestries on the south wall."

"I don't watch myself. Just old movies on weekends. I love the old black-'n-whites. Fred Astaire and Ginger Rogers, Nick and Nora Charles, and then the great political films like *Inherit the Wind* and *Seven Days in May*."

"Two of my favorites, Cody. Also *Twelve Angry Men* and two the Brits did, *The Dambusters* and *The Man Who Never Was*."

"Yes, great films." He snapped his fingers, "Plus *The List of Adrian Messenger*."

"*Advice and Consent*."

"*Strangelove*."

"But not *Failsafe*. Good film but too depressing."

"We should have movie nights."

"We can start tonight, after dinner."

"I'm game. What's for dinner?" He gestured for her to lead them back to the living area.

"I hope you're not vegetarian, " she said over her shoulder. "I should have asked."

"Only if I have to be polite. I go by the policy that animals eat animals so why shouldn't we?"

"I like that. The perfect rationalization."

Francie opened the refrigerator and pulled out several foil-covered dishes while Cody poured the wine. Francie lifted the foil off a broiling pan revealing a large slab of marinated beef.

"Ta-da! Range-fed bison." She uncovered a baking dish with baked stuffed potatoes. "Twice-cooked potatoes in their skins with bacon bits on the bottom, chives in the potatoes, and cheddar cheese on top. And to keep us moderately healthy," she said, unveiling the third dish, "French-cut green beans with toasted sliver almonds in light butter."

"I was right when I said 'yum.' But I don't see a need for the white wine you requested."

"I didn't know what I would be making when we spoke."

"That's fair."

"Besides, we can have the bubbly with desert. I picked up a tart at Pavel's. You probably don't know them yet. A bakery in P.G., and two blocks west of Fandangos on Forest. Best bread and deserts on The Peninsula."

"I came to the right place, didn't I?"

"Yes, I think you did."

XXVI

It was just turning Sunday when Cody turned into his driveway. He was on such a high as he walked into the house that he forgot to input his code until the device started beeping at him. "Something on my mind," he said as if explaining to it.

The dinner had been delicious. Afterwards, they walked out to the bluff overlooking the ocean. The fog was in as it was most of the summer, but there was a pink-orange tint to it. There was a wind off the ocean chilling the air. Cody had put his arm over Francie's shoulders to keep her warm, a gesture that seemed natural to both of them. But not enough against the cool breeze. They went back into the house.

Francie brought out two champagne glasses from the freezer, and while Cody uncorked the bottle and filled the glasses, she took out the chocolate-covered macaroons and put them in bowls atop a scoop of raspberry sherbet. She added a sprig of mint to each and carried them over to the coffee table in front of the large couch that faced the television screen revealed when she had raised the tapestry that had covered it.

After a lengthy discussion, they'd chosen the Sidney Lumet version of *Murder on the Orient Express*. After a half-hour of the film, Francie had brought the desert dishes to the sink and returned with the champagne bottle in a silver ice bucket. When she settled back on the couch, she unfolded a large lambskin throw and snuggling close to Cody, pulling it over them both.

Cody could still smell her hair when he got home. And he could vividly feel the tingle of the kiss – a brief touching of their lips – as he had left her at the door.

"Oof," he said aloud as his whole self re-played that exquisitely delicate moment. Cody closed up the downstairs, resetting the alarm, and then went upstairs to his bedroom. While he felt wide awake, even energized, he knew that with the wine he had consumed, he would fall asleep easily. And so he did, waking up surprisingly bright the next morning. He had a strong urge to call Francie, but he resisted it. He had little doubt that there was something there, but it was a relationship that needed to be nurtured. Grown carefully, not rushed. No matter his feelings, his excitement, his desire, he had to walk, not run. He had to make friends with her, moving to the deeper level over time, enjoying the various stops along the way.

He sighed, enjoying the feeling throughout his body. He went downstairs and put water on for tea. He pulled out a bagel from the freezer, defrosted it in the microwave and then put it in the toaster oven. Then the phone rang. The caller ID was blocked. He almost let it ring through to voicemail but picked it up.

"I didn't wake you, did I?" asked Francie.

"No. Good morning," he said with warm enthusiasm.

"You picked it up on the third ring was why I asked. None of my business, of course."

"There was no number on the caller ID, but I suppose there shouldn't be in your business." He chuckled. "Perhaps you were picking up on my wanting to call you and say good morning and thank you for a most delicious dinner and a wonderful, delightful, seriously pleasurable evening."

"Why didn't you call?"

"I, well, uh, I didn't want to be presumptuous."

Francie giggled. "I think we're past that stage."

"Oh good."

"I mean, that kiss last night, Cody. I never knew there could be such passion in such a filigree moment."

"Oooh, I like that. Have you written any poetry?"

"As a matter of fact I have but not the kind I'd read over the phone."

"Righto."

"Listen, I didn't call to schmooze. We forgot to watch your Soledad series last night so I did this morning. Excellent. I couldn't find anything to correct. And I'm very picky."

"I'm so pleased, Francie. You were the audience I most wanted to impress."

"And Cody, what I particularly liked was that you didn't report anything in a way that should raise the hackles of either the prison people or the inmates. It was very clean. All of the allegations were made by other credible sources, anonymous and not. Donna Mo hung herself, and Raphael Trujello did too, though not as obviously."

"I can't tell you how much your assessment means to me. You're the only one in the market who's got good news judgment, and you hit the critical points. Thank you."

"Hey, bro, this isn't about me, it's about you. I'm the one that's feeling great about the profession. What you did is real journalism."

"So when do we next get together? What time are you flying out?"

"Well, that's another reason I'm calling. As I told you last night, I have to be in Washington for the week, your big week, and I'm sorry I won't be there to celebrate your success until I get back on Friday. I was supposed to leave tomorrow flying commercial, but a friend of mine in Pebble Beach has to be in Alexandria for a dinner and offered me a ride on her Gulfstream."

"You can't turn that down. Do you need a ride to the airport?" Cody asked, trying to keep hope out of his voice. He had expected to see her before she left, but with the travel moved up a day, it didn't seem likely.

"Thank you, Cody but she's sending her driver to pick me up." There was a silence, and then she added, "I would have liked to see you before I left."

"Me too you, my dear Francie, but I understand logistics."

"I'll call you from our nation's capital. Oops, I think he's here. Take care, Cody. Hugs."

"Hugs to you, Francie. Have a good trip."

Such was the beginning of an important week. In addition to his work preparing two newscasts, Big Don had made arrangements for Cody to speak to service organizations every day that week, some breakfasts, some luncheons. He also met with reporters from the *Herald* and the two weeklies. On Wednesday, after the first piece had run, he got calls from papers in San Francisco, San Jose and Sacramento. On Thursday, Big Don had to park his secretary in the newsroom to handle the extra calls. She was there on Friday, too.

The reviews were virtually all favorable, with some blogger purists complaining that Cody had used some anonymous sources. Most everyone else understood that these people risked their lives to get the truth out. There was silence from the prison and from the Department of Corrections; hardly a surprise. A surprise was a call from Raphael Trujello's attorney, Slate Denidetto, who said his client didn't like the extra attention he was now getting but thought the reporter had done a decent job of reporting the truth.

Cody admitted to himself that Denidetto's message gave him a feeling of relief. A feeling that Francie shared when she called from Dulles Airport before she boarded a late afternoon flight to San Francisco. She would be landing at Monterey in the evening, early enough for Cody to pick her up at the airport, drive her home, and get back to the station in time for the late newscast.

He was glad his week had been so full with work that he hadn't had time to think about her. At least not obsessively. And they had exchanged a few emails and spoken by phone several times. Mostly their communications had been limited by what she was in our nation's capital to do, and that wasn't something she was allowed to discuss with Cody.

After the early evening newscast was off the air, he was called up to Big Don's office. The station manager motioned for him to sit down. "Can I offer you a drink?"

"No thanks, Don. I have to pick up someone at the airport and give her a ride home."

The man looked at Cody carefully. "Funny, I guess I never thought that you might have a personal life. I mean, already. Since you didn't really know anyone when you got here. Well, good for you. A healthy personal life provides balance. I'm sure that it will show in your work.

"Not that I expect there will be many more weeks like this one. You think your phone has been ringing off the hook, our switchboard has been swamped. I've been getting kudos from corporate. They're gonna make a big PR deal out of this, put the series up for all kind of awards. And Manda says she's been signing up new advertiser like never before."

"That's great, Don. It shows there's a market for serious journalism."

"Yessiree."

"Thank you for backing this. If you don't mind my saying, you're a credit to your position. I don't know a lot of station executives who would have shown the fortitude to do what you did. You deserve the kudos as much as I do."

"Aw shucks, Cody. We both did what we did because it was right. Now, I have some news for you. Herb Burgess is cleaning out his desk." He looked at the clock on his desk. "He should be gone by now. I told him I wanted him out by five. And I'll tell you, I kinda felt sorry for him. I mean, he knew it was coming, especially the way we promoted the heck out of your special reports. But he'd been here fourteen years, and so it wasn't so easy to let him go. But I gave him a nice severance check, so that should make him feel better."

Cody was glad the deed had been done but didn't show it. He just acknowledged what he heard with a nod of his head.

"So on Monday, I'm going to announce to the newsroom that you're the new news director. I'll call Nick Belotti over the weekend and tell him not to send anyone out before nine. Maybe you can come in a little early and be there?"

"Of course, Don. And thank you."

He waved a hand at his new news director. "I know how good you are, and that I'm lucky to have you. I intend to give you the resources to make a difference in this market. And maybe you can do some other special reports that have national impact. We'll talk about it."

"That's great. I'm excited."

"And this should please you. I told corporate about what your reports was doing for sales, and they've sent you a proposal about vesting you with stock based on increased ratings and more money on the basis of sales. Not a lot. We are the 125th market after all, but it's something. I've never seen them do anything like this before."

"Maybe journalism is going to make a comeback," Cody said with a smile.

"That would be good for everyone, wouldn't it? By the way, I'll make sure that Herb's office – your office now – will be cleaned up for you first thing Monday morning. And you let me know what you'll need up there."

"Don, what do you think about my staying in the newsroom?"

The station manager raised his eyebrows. "Hadn't thought of that. Hmm." He smiled. "Might not be a bad idea. And if you needed some privacy, you could always use the conference room. I like it, I like it. Okay, let me know what kind of set up you'd like down there. Furniture, phones, whatever."

"I will. Thank you."

"Go get your friend, Cody. Have a good show tonight, and relax over the weekend. You deserve it. You worked hard this week, and next week, you'll have a bigger plate."

Cody stood up and reached across the desk and shook Big Don's hand. There was nothing more to say. He turned and left the corner office, walking by the former news director's office. He resisted the temptation to see that it had been cleared out, not so much as giving a sideways glance at through the open door. He suspected that sales would get the space and Manda would add to her staff.

He went downstairs and checked online to see that Francie's flight had landed at SFO on time and her connection to MRY was on time. In the next hour, he would prep for the late news and he'd see her at seven.

XXVII

Their eyes locked the moment Francie turned the corner from the ramp and came into view of the airport lounge. Cody was standing off to the side, letting the crowd flow by. The plane from San Francisco had been full and Francie, when she called just prior to take-off, had told Cody not to despair, that she would be among the last off the plane. And she was. As she approached him, he took from behind his back a bouquet of yellow and red roses and handed them to her.

"Sorry, they were out of sterlings."

She took the flowers from him, leaned forward and kissed him ever so lightly on the lips. "I was practicing that touch all week," she said. "Albeit alone. I think that should be our signature." She took him by the arm and they walked toward the baggage area. "What do you think?"

"Signature? Greeting? There's so much to say in between."

"Yes," she said squeezing her arm in his.

Curiously, her bags were the first on the carousel and in five minutes they were driving out of the airport. "I love coming into Monterey," she said. "It's so easy to navigate, and in fifteen minutes I'm home."

"Good to see you, Francie. How was D.C.?"

"Oh, no surprises. Intense sometimes, dealing with the old guard. These are the people who think drones and Cruise missiles will fix everything. The problem is, they can't even identify the enemy let alone find them."

"I didn't know you were involved in that kind of work."

"I'm not really, not as an insider. Sometimes I'm asked to sit in as an outsider, to give a different perspective."

"Are you heard?"

Francie flashed a glance at him. "Sometimes, yes. But I have to break through their basic feeling of resentment. Not only because I'm not one of them, but because I'm a woman. They have a couple of women there, but they've come up through the ranks. They are totally out of touch with their feminine. At least as they express themselves. I suppose I would be too if I'd spent thirty years climbing the military ladder the way they had to. I know it's going to change over time, but I wish it would be quicker."

She smiled at him. "I missed you, Cody. Does that sound crazy? We've known each other such a short time."

"Have we only? I think maybe we've known each other a long time. We just have been out of touch for most of it."

"Hah! I like that. Suddenly it all makes sense. Sort of. But that works for me."

Francie's phone rang. "Excuse me, that must be Ariane." She pulled the phone from her pocket, looked at the display. "Yes," she said and answered the call. After a few brief pleasantries, she listened a lot, looked over at Cody once or twice, and then said good-bye.

"I thought we were going to have a nice weekend together."

"We aren't?"

"Ariane asked me to tell you that your reports stirred up a hornets' nest at Justice. They're going to take over Soledad on Sunday morning at seven. A hundred federal marshals backed by as many California National Guard."

"Oh my goodness. Can I know this?"

"Not officially, but they won't be surprised to see you and a camera person. She's going to call me tomorrow with contact information, and I'll give it to you. She doesn't think you'll get inside, but you should get some great pix, exclusively – don't you love that word!? – and maybe a spokesman at some point."

"I love exclusive," Cody said, looking over at Francie, and both of them heard the meaning in his voice.

He pulled into her driveway and got out of the car. Before retrieving her things, he opened her door and offered her his hand. She took it and stepped out, into his arms.

"I'm not one for public displays of affection, but this is private enough." They kissed softly then strongly, and after a minute, she pulled her head back. "I don't suppose you can get anyone to do the eleven for you tonight?"

"I could quit," he suggested.

"It wouldn't look good if you're going to be announced as news director on Monday morning."

"And after the scoop we get on Sunday. You're right."

Reluctantly they disengaged. Cody grabbed the luggage from the trunk and met Francie at the front door where she pressed her hand against a small glass plate. There was a click of the lock and she pushed the door open. "Ariane is really very good at what she does," she said and walked into the house.

"Where would you like these, sweetheart?"

"Oh, Cody, that sounded very nice. Uh, in my bedroom, please. Can I make you a cup of tea, or something stronger?"

"I wish I could stay...." he said before disappearing toward her bedroom, and upon reappearing continued, "...but I want to get in touch with Felice Inez tonight."

"Yes. You don't want to be scrambling for a shooter tomorrow."

They walked together to the front door. "Should I come back after the newscast tonight?"

Francie sighed. "Darling, I'd like to get some rest before I see you again. How about you come over for breakfast, say about nine?"

"Makes sense," he said, taking her in his arms again. "After all, we've known each other for ten years or so. We can wait until tomorrow." They kissed. It was a long kiss. "On second thought..."

Francie laughed and opened the door for him. "Call me when you get home, won't you?"

He pecked her on the lips. "Yes, ma'am I will." He walked back to his car, pulled out of the driveway, and waved to her as he drove away.

He pulled into the station parking lot a few minutes before eight, holding up his hand to stop Felice just as she was getting into her car.

"I was hoping I'd catch you," he said as she stepped out again. He looked around. "Are you free on Sunday morning?"

His poker voice didn't fool her. "What you got?"

He told her.

"*Madre dios*! You have really opened up a can of worms?"

"Me? Us. Anyway, yes."

"And it's exclusive?"

"That's what I've been told. So far at least. Don't tell anyone where you are going Sunday morning. Let's meet at the Denny's on Blanco near the freeway at five-thirty. That should give us plenty of time for breakfast and to get down to Soledad, shouldn't it?"

"Yeah sure. It's not like there's gonna be traffic at that hour. Will we need any special credentials?"

"I don't think so but I'll find out."

She clapped her hands. "This is big, really big." She smiled at Cody. "This is why I got into news in the first place, you know?"

"Me, too," he said. "Okay, gotta newscast to get ready. See you Sunday."

She gave him a thumbs-up and got into her car. He headed for the studio.

The newscast went off without a hitch – a good sign, Cody told himself – and he was home, with the alarm disarmed and rearmed by ten of twelve. He called Francie and could tell from the sleep in her voice that he had awakened her.

"I'm so sorry, sweetheart. Go back to sleep. I'll see you in the morning."

"Ohhhh, Cody, I fell asleep during the commercial before sports. But I saw the news."

"That's good, now go back to sleep."

"But it's so comfortable. On the couch, under the blankie." She groaned deliciously. "I don't want to get up."

"I know, darling. Sleep well."

"Cody?"

"Yes, Francie?"

"Make it eight instead of nine."

Cody laughed. "Yes, ma'am. Night-night, Francie."

"Night-night, Cody."

XXVIII

At six-forty-five on Sunday morning, Cody sat behind the wheel of his car with Felice Inez in the passenger seat, her camera in her lap, ready to get out and shoot. From where they were parked, behind a small stand of trees on the opposite side of the road fifty feet from the entrance road to the prison, they could see no discernible signs of anything out of the ordinary, but there was a palpable feeling of rising tension.

Cody first saw the man in the passenger's side mirror. A medium sized man of Hispanic appearance with brown skin and a black mustache, he was dressed innocuously in worn jeans, old boots, and an extra large untucked work shirt below a weathered cowboy hat. He wouldn't have look out of place in that part of the state except for the early hour, the bulge under the shirt at his waist, and the way his eyes darted everywhere.

By the time he reached Felice's open window, he had sized up who was in the car and what they were doing there. But to make sure, he asked, "You got something that says why you're here?" It was a fair question since the car and its occupants were as out of place as the man himself.

Cody was equally careful. "A letter from DoJ. It's in my breast pocket."

"Let me see it...slowly."

Slowly, Cody removed the letter from his pocket with his left thumb and forefinger. He held it up and then, again slowly, stretched across Felice and handed it to the man. He took the letter but didn't unfold it immediately. He looked at Cody and then through the far window at the prison several hundred yards distant. With one hand he unfolded the letter and ascertained it was what he wanted to see. He handed it back to Cody.

"Okay, here's how it will work. There's a skeleton crew on right now. The assistant warden in charge is one of our people. At seven o'clock, he's going to announce a security drill. Our people will go in. When they're in place, the assistant warden will inform the staff that they are to leave their positions and form up outside by the buses. The buses will take them down to Fort Hunter-Liggett for processing. You won't be allowed down there. You will only be allowed to go as far as the main gate, but not until the busses have arrived and our people have gotten into position. You'll get a call when you can move in." He looked at Cody who nodded and then at Felice who also nodded.

"It should all go off fairly quietly, but if you hear any shooting – and I repeat, we don't expect any trouble – but if there is any gunfire, get your butts outta there as fast as you can."

"Will there be any opportunity for an interview with any of your people, Mr. Wallace?"

The man jerked his head back at the sound of his name. He stared at Cody. He quickly decided that the reporter had better sources than he had presumed, but if he was ready to cooperate, that was really all that mattered. It was in the hands of higher authorities.

"What did they tell you?"

"I was told I could ask, and if things went as planned, if there were no unforeseen situations, that someone would be made available. I was given the name of a deputy warden named Layne Brodsky."

"Yeah, okay. If everything is cool, I'll bring him out to you at the main gate for a quick interview."

"Thank you, Mr. Wallace."

"Yeah," he said. "Keep your heads down until the busses are in and our people are on the ground. Then I'll call you to come into the gate." He recited Cody's cellphone number. Cody nodded. Wallace patted the roof of the car twice and backed away.

"I feel like I'm in a movie," Felice said, her voice low but edgy.

"No kidding. Why don't you get in the back seat on this side behind me? That should give you a clear shot of the troops arriving. When they are all inside, come back in front."

Felice slipped quietly out of the car and then got in again, sliding across the back seat where she positioned herself for the best angle.

Cody checked his watch. "If they're on time, I think we should hear them coming in about three minutes."

"So probably not a good time to take a bathroom break?"

"You're kidding?" Cody demanded, and then saw the smile on her face. He smiled back, shaking his head.

Suddenly they heard the rumble of busses.

"Early," Cody said. "Or they set their clocks wrong. Shoot everything you see."

"Got it."

Moments later, a convoy of unmarked Army green busses came along the road from behind them, proceeded by a scout car, and turned onto the prison road. The stopped briefly at the main gate and then drove forward into the prison yard. When they were out of sight and the dust had settled, Felice slipped out of the car and back into the front seat, giving Cody a quick nod.

"How long?" she asked Cody.

"If they know what they're doing, if they know who they're dealing with inside, maybe fifteen minutes. I don't think prison guards are the rebellious types. They're likely to follow orders, especially if they think it's a drill."

And it was just another fourteen minutes after Cody checked his watch that his phone rang in his hand. He connected the call. He listened and then said. "On our way." He disconnected the call and started the car. They drove down to the main gate where a guard wearing a federal uniform stepped out of the booth.

"May I see your letter, please, sir?"

Cody showed him the letter. The guard saw that it was what he wanted to see and handed it back. "Mr. Wallace said you are to meet him at the PIO office. He said you know where it is."

"I do, lieutenant, thank you," the reporter said and proceeded forward. He pulled into a parking space in front of the Press Office and they got out of the car. The door to the office opened and out stepped Lieutenant Reed.

"You?" Cody said with surprise.

Reed chuckled. "Sorry I was such a schmuck last time you were here. Had to keep up appearances." They shook hands.

"Apologies to you, too, Ms. Inez."

She laughed at him. "I can shoot here, yes?"

"Yes, ma'am. But please don't advance any closer to the main block."

"I gather things are working smoothly inside?"

"They couldn't be any quieter."

"How long have you been planning this?"

"About six months."

"I have to ask, lieutenant...are you a lieutenant?"

"Special Deputy U.S. Marshal, sir."

"And your name is Reed?"

"Yes, sir."

"So Reed, I have to ask, did our reports change the timing of your taking over?"

"I can't answer that, sir."

There came the sound of engines starting and two minutes later, the busses began to convoy out of the prison, with Felice shooting as they went by. A minute later, a civilian vehicle drove up and came to a stop next to Felice's car. Wallace got out of the passenger side and another man in a suit got out from behind the wheel.

"Mr. Howard, this is Layne Brodsky, the interim warden of Soledad, now under the control of the U.S. Marshals."

The men shook hands. Cody made sure that Felice was shooting it all, positioning herself to face the warden with the rising sun at her back.

"I know your time is short, so if you would just answer a few questions."

"No problem, Mr. Howard. But first let me say what a great job you did with your exposé. I know you didn't know we were planning the take-over, but the way you reported on the problems here I think will make it a lot easier for people to understand why we had to step in."

Cody then asked the obvious questions about when the take-over had first been conceived, what were the indications that such an action was required, how many people were involved in taking control of the prison, had there been any resistance, how would things change under federal control, and when would they expect to return the prison to state control.

Brodsky was concise and direct with his answers, something rare for a government official. But it was on the last question that he hesitated, when Cody asked how many other prisons across the country might require the same intervention.

"Uh, Mr. Howard, I can't really say. All my attention has been focused on assimilating what I needed to know about this facility and to prepare for our move today." He shot a glance at Wallace, so when the warden finished, Wallace stepped in.

"Mr. Howard, as you can appreciate, there's much still to be done here. I'm afraid the warden needs to get back to his office."

"Yes, I do appreciate you're coming out to speak to us, Warden Brodsky. Thank you."

Felice followed the men with her camera as they got into their car and drove back to the prison. When they were back inside the walls, she turned back to her reporter who was standing next to Special Deputy Reed. Cody noted that the tally light showed that she was still recording.

"Special Deputy Reed, I wonder if you might say what it was like for you during the time you were here as something of a spy. Did you feel you were in jeopardy? What would have happened if you'd been discovered to be a U.S. marshal?"

Reed smiled humbly. "Mr. Howard, I'm afraid that I'm not authorized to answer any questions from the media."

"Will you be remaining here, or will you be going on to another assignment?"

"I'm afraid that I can't answer any of your questions, sir."

"Quite a turn-around from having been the press information officer for the prison for, for how long?"

"I can answer that question. I was here for six months."

"And that's it?"

"Yes, sir. I'm sorry sir."

"I understand. Thank you."

Cody gave Felice a cut sign. "You have everything?" She nodded, holding back a smile with Reed watching her. "Then let's go. Thanks again, Reed."

"Thank you, sir, and you ma'am."

With that they got into the car, Felice driving, and slowly made their way out of the complex and to the frontage road. "It sure felt a lot better today than last time," Felice said as they merged onto the highway.

"Yes, I hope it augers well for how the prison is run."

"Do you think it will make a big difference?"

"I wish I could say yes, but probably not. Sure, they got rid of some bad apples, but the system is corrupt. I don't think it can function in today's world, with today's values." He chuckled.

"What's funny about that?"

"Nothing's funny about that. I was just remembering Twain's line – I think it was Twain – 'If you want to see the dregs of society, go down to the jail and watch the changing of the guard.'"

"That's rough."

"He had his moments."

"So what do we do with what we just shot. This is hot. Nobody else there."

"I'm going to call Don Centree at home." He looked at his watch. "Huh, it's not even eight. Well, I'll wait until eight. Are you free today? I'm going to recommend that we cut a half-hour special using what we had in the reports last week to set up what happened today."

"Sure. I figured we'd have to do something with what we shot so I didn't schedule anything?"

Cody looked over at her. "Didn't schedule or cancelled?"

"Does it matter?"

"Maybe not, but thanks."

"Like I told you, this is why I got into news."

"Good for you, Felice. I'm glad we partnered up that first day."

"Yeah. Serendipity, I guess."

"Serendipity indeed."

A few minutes later they turned off on River Road and the hour turned over on the clock. Cody called the station manager and filled him in. He did some listening and some explaining and by the time the conversation was winding down, he had a confident look on his face.

"Don is very excited. He loves exclusives. He's calling the corporate offices to get their PR machine up, on a Sunday no less, to promote the heck – he said heck – out of this. He's going to meet us at the station in a half-hour. He wants this to run from six-thirty to seven, before *Sixty Minutes*. Too bad we don't have an early news on Sundays, but at least we'll have the special."

"Oh, Cody, this is exciting. And maybe a little scary. I haven't cut a half-hour before."

He patted her shoulder. "Not to worry. I already have the script in my head. You're familiar with everything we used in the specials, and we'll use a lot from the new warden. You can use the video you shot today to cover most of him. Nothing from Reed. We're in good shape. First we'll listen to Brodsky and pull the cuts. While you're getting today's best shots, I'll rough out the half-hour."

"Will you anchor it from the desk or will you want to shoot some more?"

"I think I'll report from the anchor desk, but we don't have to do it live. I want this in the can by mid-afternoon."

"Don't you think the story is going to get out before we go on? I mean, there are lots of people, guards and staff, and their families, who will know."

"Yes, I thought about that. When I talk with Don, I'm going to suggest we do a one-minute insert after *Face the Nation*. That will get us on the air with it first, and I'll tease the special at six-thirty."

Cody waited until they reached the station and the empty newsroom to call Francie. "It was a dream shoot," he told her and then filled her in on what had happened at the prison, and his plans for the special. "Maybe you should call Ariane and invite her and Geoffrey to come to dinner with us. I want to thank her in a big way for the strings she pulled in Washington."

"I think that's a lovely idea, but I thought maybe since you were up so early, you'd like to relax tonight and then sleep in tomorrow."

"Relaxing is good, but I have to be in at nine tomorrow morning. That's when Big Don is introducing me as the new news director."

"Oh yes. Darling...?"

"Yes, sweetheart?"

"Ah, yes, I think you should consider an early retirement. I don't know that I want to share you."

Cody chuckled. "Don't think that thought didn't cross my mind. I could become a consulting detective with you. We could travel the world – or maybe just The Peninsula – digging up exciting cases."

"Perfect. I'll get some business cards printed up. Will you be home for lunch? Should I bring you lunch, Cody?"

"No thanks, Francie. I'll get a bite here. I'm going to pre-tape so we should be done by three or four. Let me know where we'll be having dinner. Wherever you want me."

"What a lovely direction. All right, I'll think about it. Call me when you get a break."

"Will do."

It wasn't but a few minutes later that the station manager arrived and easily tracked Cody down to the edit room from which the only sounds in the building were coming as he and Felice were screening the morning's footage.

"The stuff looks great. Good job, you two. I can't believe that you got this exclusively. Incredible."

"Yes, a friend of my friend who is wired in Washington made this happen. She called my friend Friday night and then made the arrangements for us to have access. It really is who you know."

"It is indeed," Big agreed, nodding his head sagely.

The station manager also agreed on the one-minute insert which Cody quickly wrote and Felice shot him at the anchor desk. They covered part of his script with some shots from that morning at Soledad and then produced a promo screen for the special at six-thirty. The insert was put into the computer and they could concentrate on producing the half-hour.

Cody was right about the editing. Because both he and Felice were so familiar with the elements used in the three special reports which were to comprise a quarter of the half-hour special, much of the work was only a matter of cutting and pasting already-edited segments. The material they shot that morning was uncomplicated.

When the special was cut, it wasn't even one o'clock. As Big Don had asked him to do, Cody called him at his club and he came back to the station to screen the special. It opened with fifteen minutes of shots from the morning, explaining what had happened during the federal take-over of the prison, and much of the interview with Warden Brodsky. The day's events were followed by the three special reports with bridges by Cody at the anchor position setting up each report. Then they came back to Brodsky with his final comments about how well the transition had gone, when he thought the state might retake control, and the kicker, how endemic the serious problems they saw at Soledad were nationwide.

Finally, with permission from the station manager, Cody took the final two minutes to extrapolate on the scope of the problem in American prisons, using material he hadn't had room for in his third special report. He closed by saying how it would probably take considerable restructuring of our criminal justice system to clear out most of the corruption and abuse that existed today.

Big Don was thrilled with what he saw. "I'm so proud of you both. Felice, I need you to put this on the intranet so the Enlaw PR department can get to work on promoting it."

"Yes sir, and I want to say that it was really a pleasure for me," Felice told him. "This is what I came to Channel 13 for. It's great. Thank you for giving us – giving me, especially – the opportunity to do this."

"I'm the one that's grateful, and to show you, I'm giving you two an extra week's vacation for this. And I know there are going to be a lot of accolades coming your way." He stood to leave, "Well, I have to get back to my wife and in-laws at the club. Call me if you need anything."

"Thanks, Don. We're going to cut a piece for the late news. I'll call Ron to let him know about it."

"Good. And I'll see you two at nine in the morning." As he left, he gave a nod of his head so that Cody would follow him. When they were out of earshot of the edit room, he reached into his pocket and pulled out his wallet. From it he extracted two hundred-dollar bills and gave them to Cody. "Buy a nice dinner for your friend tonight." Then he clapped him on the shoulder and left.

XXIX

At Francie's suggestion, they scheduled the dinner with Ariane and Geoffrey for Wednesday. After finishing up at the station, Cody went home to shower and change, and then met Francie behind the Bay School just south of Carmel Meadows to go on one of her favorite walks from Monastery Beach to the mouth of the Carmel River. While the marine layer was miles closer than the horizon, the sky above was blue and a gentle breeze off the water made it a perfect late afternoon.

"Let's not talk about work, okay?" he proposed after they had connected with a long hug and a short kiss.

"Agreed, but I do want to be somewhere to watch your special at six-thirty," said Francie.

"Righto."

"Okay then, I want to know more about the you that you haven't yet told me. For instance, I don't think I know about your family. Siblings? Where are your parents?"

"Well my friend," he began and interrupted himself. "That term certainly has taken on new meaning for me seeing you again, and all that has happened."

She reached up and squeezed his neck fondly. "Yes, for me, too."

He continued, "No brothers or sisters. An only child. Like you, I think."

She nodded.

"My parents moved to New Zealand when Cheney became vice-president. They said they had never known that there was a force of evil in the universe until he was in office, and they decided to get as far away from him as possible. My mother is a first class finagler and she managed to circumvent the regulations about people immigrating there. Something about buying a farm and hiring my father to work it."

"What kind of farm?"

"Sheep. They raise sheep."

"How, um, quaint?"

"Francie, Carmel-by-the-Sea is quaint. My parents are producing wool and food."

"Of course, excuse me, and good for them."

"Yes, and us. They love their farm, and they send me the best lamb on my birthday and at Christmas. I'll cook a leg for you next time. I guarantee you haven't had better."

"I'm getting hungry already."

At the end ofthcir walk, their appetite piqued by the salt air, they phoned ahead to Francie's favorite Chinese restaurant to put in an order for dinner to take-out. Francie drove to the Full Moon in Monterey while Cody drove home to set the table and put a couple of Sierra Nevada Pale Ales into the freezer.

Francie was back with plenty of time to spare before the start of the special.

"That's the way it is with us, isn't it? We're never late but never very early."

"I like that. And it works, doesn't it? We don't waste time."

Cody had been dishing out the food onto their plates when he stopped and pulled her into his arms. He met no resistance. "We didn't waste any time, did we?"

Francie shook her head.

"I mean, we wouldn't have been ready for each other before, I don't think."

She shook her head again. "I don't think, too," she purred. She pulled his head down to hers and they kissed. They would have continued it for who knows how long but they heard from the living room a voice on the television announcing the special report.

"Ooh," Francie said. "I don't want to miss any of it. You finish up here." And she slipped away to the living room.

"Yes, ma'am," Cody said to the vanishing figure. He finished dishing out the food and delivered the plates to the table. Then he returned for their drinks.

After about fifteen minutes, when the earlier pieces from the evening newscasts which she had already seen were airing, Francie checked her watch. "No commercials?"

"No time to sell them. We won't let that happen again. We'll have advertisers who will guarantee buys for news specials in advance."

"Good idea. You didn't want to put in PSAs?"

"I thought about it. I probably should have, but it would have entailed bringing in production people and I didn't want to hassle with that. Not on a Sunday. I actually like commercial breaks. It gives a producer time to make changes and it gives the audience time to digest."

"Are they going to air it again?"

"Probably. I can cut three or four minutes and make room for commercials."

Francie turned her attention back to the television until the program was over. "What a great job you did, Cody. I'm sure you'll get some serious recognition for it. Not only awards but job offers, too."

"You think the *Herald* will want me as sports editor."

She laughed. "Nah, you don't even like sports. But mark my words...."

In fact, it was at seven the next morning that his phone rang. It was a former network colleague who had moved over to NBC around the time that Cody had gone with ABC.

"Yo, sport, Eddie Weiss. How ya doin'?"

"Hey, Eddie, I'm well, thank you. How are things on the East Coast?"

"About the same. The networks will never change. They take themselves all too seriously. They expect the times to change with them instead of seeing that they have a totally different audience out there that doesn't use Carter's Little Liver Pills."

"Yeah, that's what it's looked like for a while."

"But that said, our news prexy asked me to find out if you might not want to come back and work for us. Your special last night got a lot of attention, at the other nets, too, no doubt. Anyway, she's looking for serious go-getters, as she put it. She said you could have Justice or the Pentagon. Three-year contract. With a signing bonus, it would be a cool million plus a nice benefits package."

"Almost as much as what I'm getting here," Cody replied.

Weiss laughed. "Yeah right. I thought you were going to say you wanted what Chelsea Clinton was making."

"It's very attractive. Not just the money and I'd love to dig my fingers into the Pentagon or Justice."

"But?"

"I'm not saying no, Eddie. I have to do some thinking. I've been finding out that there's more to life than news."

"Oh, well that can sure throw a brick through a windshield, can't it? What's her name?"

Cody laughed. "You might even know her, actually, but that's not it. Not all of it. It's funny how life works."

"Tell me."

"A couple of months ago, I would have been packing before I got off the phone with you, but a lot has happened. Not just the special, and this special lady. Friend, important friend. But for the first time, maybe ever, I have a feeling of putting down roots. It's very different. It's like there's an added dimension to my life, to who I am."

"Oh jeez, Cody, you're not going New Age Hippie on me, are you?"

"Of course not, and again Eddie, I'm not saying no. Give me a day to think about it."

"Sure, Cody, I won't tell Lizzie, but I think I know what you're going to say. And hey, pal, I'm really happy that things are going so well for you, in other ways, that you didn't jump on this offer."

"You're a pal, Eddie. By the way, may I ask how you got this number?"

"You don't want to know but I'll tell you anyway. I have a friend who's over at NSA."

"I should have guessed."

"What are friends for, right? Hey, it's pushing afternoon here. I gotta go. Lemme know by tomorrow this time what you're thinking. I don't know but that she might not sweeten the pot, but it doesn't sound like that would make a difference."

"You're right, Eddie. But again, thanks for the call, the offer, and your understanding."

It was too early to call Francie, even though he knew she was already likely stirring. Maybe even at her computer, or on a morning walk around Yankee Point. He wanted to see how things went at the station that morning, and then talk with Francie, but he already knew what his answer to NBC would be.

Cody arrived at the station in a very quiet, relaxed mood. Big Don made a big thing of the work that he and Felice had done the day before, not only catching a big exclusive, but also putting together the special. He said the station would re-run the special one night that week.

He also announced that Herb Burgess had decided he had worked enough years and had left on Friday. In his place, the station manager had asked Cody to add a second hat to his anchor work, and Cody said he would. "I offered him Herb's office – I even said I'd paint it, haha – but Cody wisely said he didn't want to be running up and down the stairs all day. So he'll be staying here with you-all."

There was applause, bordering on enthusiastic, and some talk; the mood seemed very positive. Big Don asked Cody if he might have a few remarks to make. Cody stepped forward.

"I was honored when Don asked me to take this new position. I didn't seek it. I can tell you, I wasn't sure I even wanted it. But if it helps us come together as a more cohesive news operation, then I'm all for it. One thing I am sure of and that is that I'm committed to demonstrating what quality television news is all about in this market. Let us show them how to do it right."

There were only fifteen people in the room, the news staff and some people from sales and operations, but they were clearly all on board.

"That's the kind of team spirit I've been looking for," Big Don said, raising his fist in the air. "Go get 'em." He turned and shook hands with Cody and the group dispersed. "I'm going to give Herb's office to Manda. She's going to hire a couple of new salespeople. We need them now, thanks to you."

"Great, Don. And maybe she can press some of our bigger clients to commit to supporting the kind of programming we did yesterday. I would have liked to break it up with commercials, and it's impossible to get sign-offs from agencies over the weekend."

"You and I are on the same page on that, Cody. I already spoke to her about that this morning. And she's also going to get some top-dollar sponsors for the re-airing of the special later this week."

"Good. I'll recut it with Felice to make room for the spots."

"Right. And Cody, why don't you go over to Office Depot and get yourself some new furniture. A desk, a chair, a lamp, file cabinet. I'll have maintenance expand your cubicle a few feet. I know you don't care about image, but authority benefits from image, and you have new authority."

Cody smiled. "I know you're right, Don. I'll head over there in a few minutes. And thanks."

"Thank you," Don said, and he headed back to his office.

Cody went over to Nick Belotti's desk and pulled up a chair. "Nick, I'd like you to keep all your job titles. I also think you should have some more authority. We can work that out as we go along. How's that for you?"

Belotti looked at his new boss. "I think I'm gonna like it a lot better, Cody."

"Good." Cody stood, reached over and shook Belotti's hand. "Good for all of us."

XXX

"Have you had breakfast, Mademoiselle LeVillard?"

"Not since yesterday, Monsieur Howard.

"Then I would like to take you to breakfast."

"Then I would accept, that is to say, if you are still employed and can afford such an extravagance.."

"Funny you should mention that...."

"Cody, they didn't fire you!?"

"Uh, no. I got another hat, as expected, and Don – Big Don as he likes to be called – is sending me over to Office Depot to give my cubicle the look of a little more authority."

"You don't get what's-his-name's office?"

"No, I didn't want it. I knew he could use it for sales, and I don't want to separate from the news operation. He's going to expand my cubicle a few feet. And if I need to speak privately with someone, I can use the conference room."

"I'm so pleased for you, my dear man. So pleased."

"That means we can have breakfast?

"Surely. You're at your office, should I meet you there?"

"I think I'd rather not. I'd like to protect your privacy at least for a while."

"I think that's wise."

"Why don't we meet at the Del Monte Café? It's a block south of the auto mall. Not exciting but clean and good."

"I know that place. Sure. Very clean and decent victuals."

Cody laughed. "When?"

"I can be there in fifteen minutes. That work for you?"

"Great. And remind me to tell you about the phone call I got at seven this morning."

It was her turn to laugh. "I don't think I'll have to remind you, Cody."

He laughed again. "No, you won't. Drive safe."

"See you soon."

Cody was less than seven minutes from the restaurant, so he sat down with Felice and cut down the script of the special so that there would be room for four minutes of commercials. It wasn't a complicated task; he had known he might have to make room for the spots when he wrote the piece originally.

"There," he said to her. "That will give us room for four thirty-second spots, bumpers going in and a few seconds coming back from the two breaks."

"That works easy," Felice said. "I'll have it for you to look at in an hour."

"I'll be back around then."

He drove off to meet Francie. It being mid-morning but still foggy, he took a table inside and away from the door. She arrived two minutes later and they greeted each other with their signature peck. He held her chair for her as she sat down and she favored him with an appreciative smile.

"I like when you do that, even when we're at home. It's nice."

"This may seem arcane, Francie, but I feel it's an honor to show you courtesy. Chivalry for the very special lady."

"I think you've made me blush," she said, her face indeed reddening. "I don't know if that's happened before."

Cody sat down. A waitress came to the table and recognized Francie. They exchanged greetings and she gave them menus. She offered them coffee but they both chose green tea instead.

"So, dear Cody, or should I call you Sir Cody, you chivalrous one?"

"Nah, dear is good."

The waitress was back with cups, hot water and an impressive selection of teas. When she had left, Francie told Cody that she and Ariane had come in several years earlier when they had only black tea. "Ariane, sounding very cultured as you know she can sound, suggested to the owner that they consider offering green tea, and the next time we were in, a few months later, they were doing just that."

"I like that responsiveness."

Francie nodded her agreement. "All right, what is it that you were going to tell me that I didn't have to remind you about?"

"Oh, that, well, did you ever work with a guy, or not work with but maybe know a guy named Eddie Weiss? He was with NBC, in Washington, maybe WRC."

"The name rings a bell, but an indistinct one."

"Well, I knew him when he was a producer at the network. I think he was kicked upstairs a couple of years ago."

"Was he the one who called you at seven this morning?" Francie asked, unable to keep the excitement out of her voice.

"Hey, I'm telling the story."

"Go ahead," she urged with humorous impatience.

"Yes, as a matter of fact."

"And?"

"And they offered me a job as a correspondent covering the Pentagon or Justice Department."

"Oh my goodness, Cody that's great!"

"It is?"

"Well, I mean, well yes."

"Then you're really going to like this. A three-year contract with a signing bonus and all sorts of benefits."

"How much, if I may ask?"

"One million dollars."

Francie's jaw dropped.

"A little more in the first year than a rookie in the NFL."

"That's a lot of money, Cody. And what a great job." She hesitated. "And did you tell him 'yes'?"

Cody reached across the table and took both of her hands. "I didn't, actually." Her face brightened visibly. "I told him I had to think about it. That I had met someone who was important to me, and that I had a sense of putting down roots. He said that he could maybe get me more money, but he knew that wasn't the issue."

"And? What are you going to tell him?"

"Francie, you don't want to move back East." It was more of a statement than a question.

She shook her head slowly but determinedly.

"I don't either. I have never felt better located in my life. I have a very good position at KMTY. I feel I can contribute to the community. And more to the point is that I couldn't imagine leaving you."

Tears welled up in her eyes and then began a slow roll down her cheeks. It was a while before she gently pulled her hands away to find a handkerchief in her bag. She dabbed at the tears, sniffed, and then put the handkerchief away. "Cody, darling, I would go with you to Washington, if that's what you wanted to do, but I think you are right, very right. You do belong here, and you can make a difference at the station."

The waitress arrived with the food. As she put down the plates, she looked at Francie and saw the moist eyes. "Are you all right, Miss Francie?" she asked protectively.

Francie looked up at her with a smile. "Never better, Josie. Never better."

XXXI

After breakfast, the couple drove in Cody's car to see about some new furniture for the new news director. On the short drive over, Francie asked him, "By the by, you're still carrying aren't you?"

He gave her a quick glance and returned his eyes to the road. Then he did a scan around the car. And another.

"I am. I thought maybe I didn't have to anymore, but I knew that you'd get on my case." He smiled. She saw it.

"I know you are. I felt it on your belt."

"Yes, and I'm glad you are. It's not about being a poster pair for the NRA. You just don't know who is out there. You're increasingly a public figure. You step on toes, some hard. The people you hurt may not be the immediate victims but family or friends. They may try to get even."

"I hear you, Francie. I don't particularly like the idea, but I guess that's the world we live in. That people think that violence is going to salve their ills." He turned into a parking space. "Maybe we can do some shooting together. I'm sure you have some things you could teach me."

"Yes, Cody. Let's watch each other's backs."

Cody couldn't help but crack a smile. Francie managed to keep a straight face for all of two seconds but then laughed. "You are incorrigible, in a darling way."

They spent fifteen minutes picking out appropriate furniture for Cody's new "office" and then he drove her back to her car. "I'm going to run home for a couple of minutes. I left Eddie Weiss' number there and I don't want to keep him hanging. I also want to call him from home."

"Cody...." Francie began with some concern in her voice.

"Yes, sweetheart?"

She took a deep breath and let it out. "Please take care."

Though he tried not to show it, he was concerned by her evident distress, and when he said, "Of course I will," he did so to mollify her. They exchanged a quick kiss and soon were on their on separate ways.

As Cody drove up to his house, he noticed an older blue Ford 150 pick-up parked across the street from his house. It appeared to be empty, and Cody's scan of the area showed no one in sight. Still, he felt uncomfortable. He thought he had seen that same truck on Del Monte Boulevard when they left the restaurant to go buy the furniture. Six weeks ago he might have dismissed his sense of alertness as part of an over-active imagination, but not today. Not after what he had learned from Francie and Ariane. And Deki-san.

He turned into his driveway and opened the garage door with his clicker. As he began to nose his car in, he saw his friend moving toward him from his house. He got out of the car and walked out of the garage. Deki had already crossed Cody's driveway. As he walked out to greet his neighbor, the thought crossed Cody's mind that he had gotten there quickly.

He was still several yards from Deki when he saw a man run from behind the pick-up and across the street toward him, stopping at the end of his driveway. He was a total stranger – a middle-aged white man, unprepossessing in jeans and a sweatshirt except that he was pointing a gun at Cody.

There was no chance for Cody to reach for the Colt in his ankle holster, so he used the only other weapon he had. In a startlingly even voice he said, "I think you must be mistaking me for someone else. I've never bothered anyone enough to get them this angry at me."

"Yes you did. He told me what you did, and this is for him." The gun shook slightly as he pulled the trigger. Being that he was only fifteen feet away, the movement of the gun did nothing to change the path of the bullet.

But something did. It was difficult for Cody's eyes to interpret the blue blur before them but his full attention was on the fact that the bullet did not strike him. The natural order of events had gone awry.

Suddenly, from outside of the intense, private realm that was Cody's stage, Francie entered at the left edge of his field of vision. He heard her shout. "Hey!" It didn't matter what she had said, just that it drew the would-be killer's attention away from Cody, so he didn't pull the trigger again. Instead he turned toward the shout.

He hadn't finished turning toward her when she fired her own gun twice in quick succession. The first magnum slug from her S&W .357 shattered the killer's right hand and plowed up his forearm, leaving his gun dangling from his useless fingers. The second bullet hit the man squarely in the chest, separating his xiphoid process from the rest of his sternum before finding relatively clear going as it shredded several heart muscles and exiting between of third and fourth ribs on his left side.

In such moments of intense chaos, the mind works in mysterious ways. Cody noted that Deki was standing stock still, but not where he'd been when the shooting started. His mind also recalled to him that he had seen that flash of the blur after seeing the bullet leave the killer's gun. And in that instant, Cody registered that the blue was the same indigo color as Deki's shirt.

His mind done for the moment, Cody's eyes took over as he witnessed the body of the would-be killer slowly crumbling to the ground. Not ready to move himself for a moment, Cody watched Francie walk carefully toward the dead man, her gun, held in both hands for steadiness, pointing ever lower as she tracked its target.

He watched as Francie closed on the corpse. Without taking her aim off the body, she carefully nudged the dead man's gun away from what was left of his hand until it was well out of conceptual reach. It was only then that she stood up from her shooting crouch and let her shoulders relax. The gun pointing down at the ground, her thumb flicked on the safety.

She turned and stared, first at Deki, shaking her head once in curiosity and confusion, before shifting her attention to Cody. "You all right?" she asked. There was a noticeable tremor in her voice, as there should have been. No one is ever cool in such a situation, not after virtually blowing away a human being, regardless of the justification.

Cody managed to nod his head. Then, "Yes, thank god, Francie. You knew something was wrong." He didn't have to ask. Suddenly his shock freed him and he walked over to her, enfolding her in his arms, tears flowing down both their cheeks. They held each other for what seemed a long time, though it wasn't but a half-a-minute. When they heard the siren, they released each other and turned toward Deki.

He slowly took a couple of steps toward them and stopped. "I called the sheriff when I saw his truck. There was something wrong. I thought I could call you at your office but then I saw your car. I came out to warn you but then you walked out of your garage."

The siren grew louder and quickly louder and soon flashing lights accompanied the sound to the scene. An unmarked patrol car raced up the street, coming to a sudden stop fifty yards away. Deputy Ursula DeVine quickly opened her door, exited her car, taking a position behind the open door, her gun pointed at them. "Put the gun down on the ground, ma'am, very carefully.

Francie complied.

"Ursula, it's all right. She's a friend of Bogie's and mine," Cody told her urgently. He pointed at the corpse. "She saved our lives. She shot this man who tried to kill me."

The deputy looked over the situation for a long moment and then pulled her gun back but didn't holster it. She scanned the area, her eyes resting on the blue pick-up. As she walked toward it, she again raised her gun. Carefully she looked inside and seeing it was empty, she lowered her pistol and walked over toward them, her eyes taking in the obviously-dead man, continuing her 360-degree scan.

"He was alone?" she asked.

"Yes," answered Deki.

"You're all all right. No one hurt?"

"Yes we are," Cody told her. "Thank goodness. Thanks to Francie.."

He might have added "and to Deki-san" but he hadn't figured that part out yet.

She stood about ten feet from the body. "Do you know this guy, Cody?"

"Never saw him before that I know of, except..."

"Except?"

"I think I might have seen his truck on Del Monte Boulevard about a half-hour ago."

The deputy peered at the body. She said to Francie with awe in her voice,"You did this?"

"Yes."

"Very nice shooting, if I may say," throwing a smile in her direction. "I trust you have a permit for that gun."

"Yes, deputy, issued by Sheriff Spivac."

"Good. You can retrieve your weapon though I expect they'll want to check. Pro forma, you know."

"Yes I do. Thank you." Francie stooped, picked up her gun, and returned it to the holster on the back of her belt.

The deputy pulled a phone from her belt and pressed a button. She was connected with dispatch immediately. "This is Deputy Ursula DeVine. I'm at 308 North Palm Drive in Carmel between Third and Pine. There's been a shooting. The scene is no longer active. We have a dead man who was killed after he tried to murder the resident."

She listened briefly. "Yes, the situation is secure. We'll need a kill-team." She listened again. "Right. Correct. No sirens. And please patch me through to the sheriff."

The wait wasn't more than five seconds. "Sheriff, Deputy Ursula DeVine." He must have been aware of Deki's call. "He's all right. So is his neighbor, and Francie LeVillard. She was a hero, sir. She took down the man who tried to kill Cody Howard....Yes sir...Yes sir. ...Right, I'll tell them." She pushed a button on her phone and returned it to her equipment belt. "The sheriff told me to tell you that he's on his way over."

"Ursula, I hate to put on the reporter's hat, but can I call the station and get a crew here."

She gave him an indecipherable look which turned into a reluctant smile. "I hate it when the press shows up, but I guess I don't have much of a choice. Do you have your own phone?"

Cody laughed. "Yes ma'am, I do," he said, taking it from his jacket pocket. "Thank you." He punched in the hotline number. He was pleased to note that it was picked up on the first ring.

"Nick, Cody. You need to send a shooter – oops, wrong term – camera person over to my house. There was a shooting here....No, everyone's all right. Well, not the shooter....No idea who he is, was....The sheriff's people may be able to find out....I'll cover this story, but get Ron to anchor the news, both the early and the late newscasts. It will be all that I can do to report what happened....Nick, Nick, I'm all right. Yes I was the target, I don't know why, but I hope to find out before we go on the air. I'll fill you in when I get back. Probably a couple of hours." He looked up at Ursula. "Get that camera out here fast, before the cops mess up the scene....Yes, that's right; North Palm Drive between Third and Pine. And don't call unless it's really important. I'm going to be busy here. Thanks." He disconnected the call.

He stepped over to Francie and took her into his arms again. She wrapped hers around him. He said to her softly, "Oh my dearest Francie, I don't have the words to tell you all that is inside me."

She rubbed his neck. "I'm glad you're not doing the newscasts to-night, Cody. I need to be in your arms."

"Me too, sweetheart." He looked at Ursula DeVine. "How is it that you were the first on the scene, Ursula? Not that I'm not terribly relieved. I can't imagine what might have happened if it was someone who didn't know me."

"Per the sheriff, I had entered your address in my onboard computer as a priority. When the call came in, I was over by the hospital, and I came code three."

"Serendipity," Cody said to Francie.

In fifteen minutes, an ambulance, a sheriff's tactical van, a marked and an unmarked car were parked in the street. Two EMTs had jumped out of the ambulance and unloaded their gurney, but a fast look at their customer slowed their rush. Deputy DeVine went over to confer with the two uniformed and two plainclothes officers. Soon they dispersed, the uniforms setting about marking the scene with tape around the perimeter and marking chalk circles around the empty shell casings.

DeVine and the two in plainclothes walked over to Cody and Francie. Introductions were made, and then with Roy Deki who hadn't moved from his spot since the three shots were fired. Two bullets were accounted for, but the first had followed an impossible trajectory that must have somehow passed by Cody by inches; very few inches.

It was quickly established that the bullet from the dead man's gun had lodged itself in a four-by-four stud in the back wall of Cody's garage. Without any overt communication among the three people who had witnessed the shooting, there was a tacit agreement not to discuss how it was that the killer had missed his target. The forensics people simply inferred, not unreasonably, that the man hadn't aimed right, or that the muzzle of the gun had moved an inch when he had pulled the trigger. They'd been doing this work and casually could say they'd seen it all. But for Francie, Deki, and Cody, the facts needed to be talked out after the deputies had done their work.

Fergy and Felice both arrived at the corner of Third and North Palm Drive around the same time as the forensics team. They had covered plenty of crime scenes and knew how to get their shots without getting in the way of the investigators. When the deputies gave him leave, Cody moved away from the action and gave them the facts. He would have liked to leave Francie and Deki out of the story to protect their privacy, but it would have left holes too big to go unfilled. Francie and Deki both understood.

The sheriff drove up after Cody had sent Fergy back to the station with his and Felice's video and to report to Nick and Ron. Felice would stay in case there were any late breaks, and in case Cody wanted to report from the scene. After he was briefed by his investigators, the sheriff called Cody and Francie aside.

"We've got an ID on this guy. His name was Mort Schleimann. He lived in an apartment complex in new Monterey."

"Any connection with the prison? Relatives on the staff? People inside?' Francie asked. "Oh, sorry, Cody. It's your story."

Cody chuckled. "You asked all the right questions, my inestimable colleague. You know, Sheriff, that he said he was doing this for 'him' but he didn't say who the him was."

"We've got someone at the place now asking around." The phone on the sheriff's belt buzzed. He took the call. "Yeah?" He listened. "Damn. Oh damn." He sighed. "Bring him in. Let's make sure we get everything from him when he's able to talk."

He put the phone back on his belt. "You'll never guess who his roommate was."

Francie nodded her head but didn't say anything. The sheriff stared at her.

"You think you know? How could you know?" He shook his head in disbelief. "It was Herb Burgess. They went to this guy's apartment," he said, nodding in the direction of the corpse that was just then being wheeled away on the gurney. "They could hear what sounded like moaning inside but they couldn't get anyone to answer the door. They were about to break it down when the building manager showed up and opened it for them. Burgess was incoherent, all but passed out on the couch with an empty bourbon bottle next to him."

Francie nodded her head, and then reached over and pulled Cody to her. He didn't resist.

"You're not surprised, Francie?" The sheriff asked. "How did you know?"

She pulled back slightly from Cody and said to him, "Bogie, this has to be off the record since it doesn't matter, but when I was leaving Cody at the restaurant, I had this gut feeling that there was something wrong. I don't think I'd seen the blue truck or that guy, but my instincts were lit up bright and flashing red. That's why I followed Cody here. On the way, I asked myself who could possibly want to do him harm. The prison people were obviously possibilities, but I would have thought they would have acted last week. And from what we were hearing, they weren't as upset with Cody as they were worried about keeping their jobs anyway.

When I drove up and saw Deki-san crossing the driveway, and then Schleimann walking over with a gun, I got a picture in my mind of Burgess. Maybe it was because we were picking out furniture for his replacement. Maybe it was because this was the first morning that he wasn't going to the office that it precipitated this." She shrugged her shoulders. "I can't tell you anything more than that. I jumped out of my car and pulled my gun but not in time to stop him from shooting. Then I shouted to turn him away from Cody and to give me a bigger target." She winced. "Ooh, that sounds bad."

The sheriff patted her on the back. "Thank God you did, Francie. Thank God you did."

XXXII

"A serious reporter never wants to be part of his story," Cody began his report for the KMTY newscast. "Especially with what happened to me today. But I was there. I was the reason for the story, and so I must report it to you.

"Last Friday, Herb Burgess, the former news director at our station resigned. This morning, I was named to replace him. From what the sheriff's investigators have learned, Burgess was not happy about leaving his job and after drinking heavily, he had communicated his unhappiness in strong terms to his roommate, a man named Mort Schleimann. Burgess and Schleimann had been friends for many years and roommates for the past six.

"Schleimann took it upon himself to avenge Burgess' departure by trying to kill me. It is believed that he followed me in his truck this morning while I was running errands, and then drove to my house. When I got out of my car in the garage, I saw him at the end of the driveway with a gun pointed at me. I told him I must be the wrong person since I'd never done anyone enough harm to want to kill me. He said, 'Yes you did. He told me what you did, and this is for him.' Then he fired a shot that just missed me.

"A local consulting detective whom I know had driven over to my house and had witnessed the shooting. She was armed. She called to Schleimann. When he pointed his gun at her, she shot him.

"Mort Schleimann died at the scene. No one else was injured. Investigators say they have more questions for Burgess but expect no new developments. I'm Cody Howard, Channel 13 News."

XXXIII

"Jeez, Cody, you really are all right?" Eddie Weiss had called shortly after the newscast had ended at five-thirty.

"Yes, shaken but no bullet wounds."

"Jeez," he said again, "You're in Afghanistan for six months and nothing. You're in bucolic Carmel and bam! What's happenin' in the world?"

"It's crazy, isn't it?"

"Cody, I learned from our affiliate in Salinas that the detective who shot the guy was none other than Francie LeVillard, who, as you know, used to work for us in Washington and New York. I think I even met her a couple of times." He gave Cody a chance to comment but when nothing was said, he continued. "She was one great journalist, and when I checked up on her, I found that she's now one great detective."

"Consulting detective," Cody corrected.

"And apparently one great shot." More silence. "So putting one and one together, I'm guessing that she might be the reason that you aren't in a hurry to jump at our offer." He paused. "Even if we jump it up. Say, double it?"

"Funny thing, Eddie, but the reason this came down the way it did was that I was coming home to tell you 'Thank you but no thank you.' Yes, the DoJ or the Pentagon would be real plums and the money is mind-boggling, but – and this is off the record, strictly between you and me – she has roots here. They go deep. I know that being the news director at the second-place station in the 125th market doesn't sound like much, but, especially as the last week has shown, it's more than enough for me. I'm planting my roots right here, too.

"I greatly appreciate the offer. I think it would have been a great opportunity but I know you can find someone else who is maybe younger and would better fit in with the audience you're trying to develop."

"I don't suppose if I told you we were going back to real journalism that would make a difference?"

"I'm delighted to hear that, Eddie, you know I am. It's what the country truly needs. A strong Fourth Estate. That's what I'm doing here as well."

"All right, pal. I understand. I really do. For what it's worth, I think the offer will be on the table if you ever change your mind."

"Thanks, Eddie. And good luck."

"You, too, Cody. And regards to Francie."

"Night, Eddie."

Cody ended the call. He'd been holding the phone slightly away from his ear so Francie could hear both sides of the conversation, though with Weiss' strong voice, she would have heard anyway.

"You did good," she said to him. She had been sitting on the couch next to him but now she climbed onto his lap. She put her arms around his neck. "Though I almost laughed when you corrected him about me being a 'consulting detective'." She kissed him. "And I'm glad you didn't use my name in your report. I know the other station and the papers will, but it was classy for you not to. I think it also only enhances your credentials as a journalist, at least with the people in this market who know the difference."

"Yes, it was right."

There was a knock on the door. "That should be Deki-san." Francie got off his lap and Cody stood up. "Curious, he usually rings the bell."

Francie was suddenly alert but then she relaxed. "Maybe his arms are full." She walked over to the door and checked through the security hole. "It's your neighbor all right, and with food. I'm glad he got rid of the restaurant so that he could serve us." She laughed and opened the door wide. "*Kangei*, Deki-san. Welcome."

"*Watashi wa koeidesu.* I am most honored to be welcome." Even with his arms filled, he managed a bow. Francie bowed and then relieved him of a tray heaped with different treats.

"*Domo arigatozaimashita*, Deki-san," said Cody who had joined Francie at the door to help. "Although thank you doesn't begin to express my humble gratitude."

"Mine, too," Francie echoed. "I don't know how you did it but you saved this dear man's life."

The tray of food was put in the middle of the dining room table with plates and napkins and glasses. As they were filling their plates, Cody said to his neighbor, "With your having been in the restaurant business for so many years, you must know the expression, 'sing for your supper,' yes?"

"I have heard that expression, yes."

"Well, tonight you bring us this sumptuous buffet AND you have to do the singing."

"Deki-san, you must explain what happened out there. What we saw," Francie said, putting her hand on Cody's shoulder. "What did you do? How did you do it?"

"Yes, I know I must sing, and I will after we eat."

"*Doi shite.* Or as we'd say among friends, deal," said Francie.

Deki was seated at the head of the table and Francie and Cody sat on either side of him, facing each other.

Though the nights were cooling off earlier, the house was still warm and warmer still with the friendship at the table. The food enhanced the atmosphere. There were the traditional sushi and sashimi, salads, and other treats, complemented by plum wine and Sierra Nevada, which Deki now preferred to Japanese beer.

When they could eat no more, Cody carried the remaining food into the kitchen, and with Francie, wrapped it and put it into the refrigerator. Then they washed and dried the tray and left it on the counter.

"We have some light pastries, Deki-san," Francie announced as they walked over to the living room and ensconced themselves in softer furniture, "but let us digest that exceptional meal."

"While I do some singing?"

"Yes," Cody answered him, "but first, I have to tell you how important it has been, all that you have told me about. What shall I refer to them as, the Eastern ways? You have been most generous with your time and sharing, and literally, it has changed my life."

"Yes, thank you," Francie told him, "for it has changed my life, too."

"We are one," Deki-san said, bowing his head to them.

"You need to explain to me what happened out there," Cody said, coaxingly. "I saw the bullet leave the gun. It was aimed right at my chest. It couldn't miss. There wasn't time to get out of the way. I didn't move, and yet the bullet missed me. How? And why do I think I saw a flash of blue, just like the color of your shirt."

"You did see the blue flash of color. It was my shirt that you saw."

Cody narrowed his stare at the man. "You were on the left side of the bullet's path and then you were on the right. You moved when the bullet was fired?"

"Just then."

"And?"

"You must understand a basic principle of physics which is that we can't see energy until it slows down to become light. And it must slow down much further to become matter. We can use energy to move matter. The great martial artists throw their opponents without actually touching them."

"Are you saying that you were able, using your energy, to change the trajectory of that bullet after it left the gun?"

"That is what happened." Deki saw that wasn't enough of an explanation. "I crossed his target line just as he pulled the trigger. That was the blue flash that you saw. In doing so, I created an energy wave that drew the bullet about eighteen inches to the left of where it was headed. It flew harmlessly past your right arm and hit the stud in the back of your garage.."

"But that seems beyond imagination."

Deki looked at him. "Not beyond imagination. I know it appears incomprehensible to you, but it is actually the mind at work. The energy of thought, focused, can do almost anything. Most people aren't aware of their own power, which is a good thing because the world is not ready for such power. We don't have the morality to move mountains, as it might be said. It is quite new for me, too, but this morning I had to act."

Cody had an inspiration. "You saw Schleimann. You knew why he was here. You called 911 but then you saw they wouldn't arrive in time so you acted." He shook his head as if he didn't know where the thought had come from. "Is that right?" His expression said he knew it was. "But how did I know that?"

Deki remained silent.

"You put the thought in my mind, didn't you? Oh my goodness." Cody sat back on the couch, looking alternatively out the window toward the backyard but seeing nothing, and at Deki, and trying to fathom what he was hearing – and experiencing – but which was far beyond the bounds of what he had ever known.

"So you understand what we are capable of. But until we also reach a level of consciousness where we can use such powers productively – even safely – they will not be revealed to us."

"Thank goodness," Cody said, shaking his head at the thought. He stared hard at Deki-san. "This is like what Obi-Wan Kenobi did in the *Star Wars* film and Luke in *Return of the Jedi*. They were able to control lesser minds. But it's not just the stuff of movies. It's real, isn't it?"

"Yes it is. It is a power we all have, and it will grow within you because you are an old soul who is noble in conscience. I used it to save your life this morning because of who you are and what you still have to do."

"Deki-san, you have upended me. My world is suddenly very different." He laughed. "I had an image – I had it, you didn't give it to me – and it's interesting that I can tell the difference. The image was from the first *Superman* movie, when Superman reversed the Earth's rotation to go back in time to save Lois Lane. He wasn't supposed to do that but he did." He laughed again. "Amazing, just amazing."

"I don't think this is completely new to you, is it, Francie?

She shook her head. "Our friend is very advanced. He has the courage to pioneer to levels of awareness and focused energy that are beyond what most people have witnessed. But I have been aware of them for a while. He's right. The world is not ready for people to have this power, but we are moving in that direction. I saw it before today, and we will see increasingly more of it. It may be what saves us."

Cody raised his eyebrows. "I get that. Someone with this knowledge blocking a terrorist act."

"Yes," said Francie, squeezing Cody's hand. "Like what Deki-san did today. He stopped a terrorist."

He sat thinking for a long moment and then asked, "So what's next, Deki-san?"

The man smiled softly. "We don't know, do we?"

XXXIV

Cody felt a need to get into the office early the next morning. He first checked in with Nick Belotti.

"There's going to be a follow-up on the shooting," Cody said. "I'd like to extract myself from the story as quickly as possible. Let's have one of the reporters cover it. I'd like to get back to anchoring."

"Right," said Belotti, with a different tone in his voice. Some of the distance he exhibited was due to the fact that Cody was his new boss, but there was more. There was respect for the fact that this man had cheated death. And unless one had been in the military, which Belotti had not, or been a doctor, also not, one was not likely to have met people who had been given a second chance. He peered at his colleague.

"What was it like, Cody? Did you think...did think that you were going to die?"

It surprised the journalist when he realized he hadn't asked himself the question. Myriad thoughts raced through his mind trying to get his attention. "It's interesting, Nick, but you know, I didn't. I don't really understand why. There wasn't a lot of time to think, really. All of maybe ten seconds. And, I'd prefer that you not repeat our conversation, it's something very private, but I actually saw the bullet as it left the gun."

"You're kidding!?"

"It was heading right for my chest."

"Holy crap!"

Cody shook his head in amazement as he played back the events in his mind. "I don't know how fast thoughts travel, but I had this sense that – how do I put this? – a sense that I would know what I had seen. That somehow I would remember this. Which meant that I would be alive still?"

"Were you afraid?"

"No. There probably wasn't time for fear. It was all so fast."

Belotti shook his head. "What an incredible thing. You spent all that time in war zones, ducking bullets and bombs, and someone almost kills you in your own driveway in pastoral Carmel. You ought to write a book about your experiences, Cody. I mean, not just the shooting, but what you've seen. I think a lot of reporters would gain something from your observations."

Cody chuckled. "I'd just like a couple of weeks off to walk the beaches of Kauai. But I appreciate the thought. Maybe someday."

Belotti nodded his head. "Yeah, think about it. At least write down some notes. About what happened yesterday, and also, Felice was telling me about when you were at Soledad, doing those interviews, and just what it felt like. And not to tell you what to say, but I gotta think that young reporters would benefit from explaining when you cut a piece, you don't bring your own feelings to the editing room. You know, like how you felt about that woman from Corrections or that cartel leader. A lot of people would have made them look bad or worse. You let them tell their side of things."

"Thanks, Nick. I appreciate what you're saying and I'll take your advice about making some notes while this stuff is fresh in my head."

"Yeah, oh, and Big Don said to stop up when you come in."

"On my way."

He walked past his cubicle and was pleased to see that it had already been expanded. He also saw that the furniture he had ordered a single tumultuous day earlier had arrived. Upstairs he found the door to the station manager's office open. He knocked on it as he walked in. The man stood up and reach his hand across the desk. Cody shook it. "Glad to see you're in one piece, Cody."

"Thanks, Don. Good to be in one piece."

"I can't imagine what you went through."

"I haven't parsed it yet myself."

The men sat down. "I know this isn't going to be a regular thing," Big Don said with a small laugh. "Otherwise I could get rid of our promotion department. But seriously, what's happened in the last, what, five days has been a whirlwind. Great visibility for Channel 13. Corporate just loves it. And they want to exploit it."

Cody grimaced.

"I know, I know, but it would be foolish not to make the most of it."

"I understand. Stations, and the networks, try to make the personalities bigger than the news. I think that takes away from the importance of clean journalism."

"Yes, but. And the 'but' is that the prison series, the feds taking it over, and the shooting yesterday, even though it was totally – well, mostly totally – unrelated to the Soledad coverage, garnered a lot of outside interest and you were at the center of it all."

Cody nodded.

"So I won't be ham-handed about this, but I think you should make yourself available if the appropriate interview requests come your way."

Cody chuckled. "Of course I will, Don. You sound like you know already that some might be in the pipeline."

The station manager held up a palm. "I didn't solicit any, I promise you, but if your name gets out, it's good for the station, for the ratings, for building your reach. Showing what good journalism is all about."

"You're right. I'm on board with you."

"Good. I knew you would be. Your humility is honest, but you also know how to further our mutual aims." He sat back in his chair, signaling the end of their conversation. Cody stood up to go. "And Cody," he said before his anchorman had left the room.

"Yes, sir?"

"Personally, I'm glad it's turned out this way."

"Why thank you, Don. So am I. For both of us."

Downstairs, Cody had been moving out the old and moving in the new furniture, emptying and filling drawers, when his cellphone rang. The caller ID showed blocked but with a code that let him know it was Francie calling from her cell.

"Hello, sweetheart."

"Hi, you getting off for lunch?"

"If that's an invitation to have it with you, you know my answer is yes."

"Do you have your sneaks in you car?"

"Yes again."

"I was thinking we could do the Monastery Beach walk and then get a bite at Erik's. Have you back before one. Is that enough time for you?"

"That works. It's a quiet day with a number of pieces by the reporters."

"Okay, come on."

"Where shall I meet you. France?"

"In the parking lot."

"Which parking lot?"

"Darling, I'm about ten feet from the main entrance to KMTY."

"Then I shan't dawdle."

He told Belotti he'd be on his cell and went out the back door to get his sneakers out of his car. Then he walked about the corner of building and got into Francie's car. He leaned over to her and gave her their signature peck. She put her hand behind his head and pulled him back for a longer kiss. When she was done, she let him go.

"I know what I said about being a private person, but sometimes that marvelous peck is just not enough."

"I know what you mean," Cody said, his voice slightly roughened. "Maybe we should just go to my place and, uh, talk."

"Oh, but darling, you have your sneakers. It would be a waste."

She laughed and drove them toward the beach. "And besides, there really are some things I want to, uh, talk about with you."

"Like you think we'd have more time together alone if we moved to Washington?"

"No, that wasn't one of the things. Although I thought about it. I don't think they'd keep you at Justice or the Pentagon. What did you call it the other day, the five-sided funny farm? That was very funny. No, I think they'd soon want you traveling, maybe like, who was that for CBS...Charles Kuralt."

"Truth be told, that would be a wonderful gig. You and me touring America in a Winnebago."

"The touring part I would like, but not the Winnebago. I only rarely sleep between metal walls, like on a plane. Anyway, we're not moving. Are we?"

Cody shook his head. "I had a good conversation with Don Centree this morning. Every time we talk I find more substance in the man."

"Neat."

"And I got a most provocative suggestion from Nick Belotti."

"Of all people. He's coming around, too, is he?"

"Yes, yes he is. But full stop, you had things you wanted to talk to me about. What Nick said can wait."

They were at the long light at Rio Road. Francie looked over at Cody with deep affection. She said softly, "You really are a good fit for me, Cody. So present. So considerate."

"So, you're coming around, too?" he asked and they laughed together again.

They started on their walk and in a few minutes were mounting the bluff that rose a hundred feet above waves laving the beach below.

"I don't know if I told you, I think I did, that I sent a note to Beth – Beth Rosemont – a few weeks ago, to thank her for re-introducing us."

"Yes, you did. Did you hear from her?"

"I did. This morning. She called. She said she had seen in the news about the shooting and had tried to call you but either the call didn't go through or she had mis-dialed."

"No, I didn't hear from her. How is she?"

"She was genuinely concerned about you, Cody. She said she hadn't heard from you in ages, and the last time you had talked you – just after you had arrived in Monterey and you weren't into your house yet – that you had sounded terrible. Her word. Then when she saw the report of the shooting, she called to make sure you were okay."

"My goodness, what did you say in your note?"

Francie shrugged. "Nothing effusive. I just thanked her for getting us together, that we'd had dinner a few times, and were enjoying each other's company."

"That was it?"

"Yes, since that was what it was, well maybe not by the time I sent the note but at the beginning. I didn't think it was my place to tell her how serendipitous – there's that word again – was your moving out here and our getting together. I knew where you were with me, but I didn't know where she was with you. If you get my meaning."

"I do. I think you handled it perfectly. It was over between us but there were times when neither of us was absolutely sure that it was, but it was never at the same time. Moving out here was defining, though."

"That was my sense of it. Anyway, I told her there was no need for her to worry, that you were doing well, very well. I told her about the Soledad coverage. And about the shooting."

"Did she press you on the details?"

"Yes."

Cody didn't have to pursue the issue. "Did she sound good to you?"

"The truth? I think she feels a sense of loss. She may not have wanted you, but she didn't want to lose you. I didn't give her enough information that she would know about us, but the job and the distance, and not being able to get you on the phone. I think she inferred that you wouldn't be available to her, not the way you were."

"Ahso. Well good. The break will do her good, I think. It should be an impetus for her to move herself forward, whatever that might mean for her."

"That's nice," Francie said. They continued their walk, descending the long stairs that divided the state parkland from the private property on which sat the very expensive homes of Carmel Meadows, and led down to the path above the beach.

"Cody, I also wanted to talk to you about shooting that man. I wanted to make sure that I didn't seem to process what happened too quickly. Without feeling it; not being upset by it."

He turned her to face him and took both her hands in his. "Sweetheart, I thought you were magnificent."

"Did you, Cody? You weren't concerned that I didn't seem more upset about what happened? I mean, I had just killed a man. Should I have gotten hysterical?"

"Oh darling you killed a charging animal. He would have shot Deki-san after me. What you did was truly heroic, drawing his fire to yourself the way you did and then ending the killing."

"I shouldn't be upset that I took a human life?"

"Francie, John Donne is famous for having said, 'Any man's death diminishes me,' but he was from another time. You've seen a lot of life, both as a journalist and as a consulting detective. The range of human life is very wide. Not all human beings are worth maintaining or protecting. Some lives need to be ended. Think of those ISIS psychopaths who beheaded the two American journalists and slaughtered thousands of captives. Some people are too dangerous to others to live in society. You stopped that man from killing two people in the next five seconds."

Francie nodded. "I'm glad you see it that way. I knew it was right. I just didn't want to seem blasé about it."

"You didn't seem at all blasé, Francie. Just remarkably cool." He added, "If you are worried, I think you should talk to Deki-san. He would be a better guide for you through your thoughts. But as far as I'm concerned, thank goodness you were there. Thank goodness for your experience that provided the presence you needed to be heroic."

"Thank you, Cody. I've told you about having to shoot those Russian mobsters."

"Yes, and how many lives did you save then. Five or six by my count."

Francie nodded. "Okay, thank you. I just wanted to make sure. Now let's change the subject."

"Wait before we do, I just wanted to say that I was glad you brought this up because I had a funny thought which seemed totally inappropriate, but we journalists have a strange sense of humor, don't we?"

"I'm not sure," she replied with a chuckle. "How strange are we talking about?"

"Well, I was thinking how funny it would have been if when Deki-san had been hosing the blood off the driveway last evening, someone would have complained about him violating the drought regs."

"Oh, Cody, you're terrible." She punched him playfully in the shoulder. "But it is wonderful black humor. So now we can move on, yes?"

"Yes, darling."

"Okay, your turn. What did your new pal, Nick Belotti, say to get your attention?" They started walking the path again, her hand through his arm.

"It was very interesting. He thinks I should write a journalism book, about my experiences, how to handle news stories. I'm extrapolating now from what he said, but a book that would include real stories, about me and other journalists, that would provide guidance about how to do our jobs. How to fulfill our calling."

"Cody, that's a great idea. I know we don't need the money, but turning down that million-and-a-half, and the prestige of the network job, you gave up a lot. This book could earn it back, not just the money, but the visibility. Plus you'd be helping to produce a stronger Fourth Estate, and we certainly need that. I think it's a great idea."

"Do you think it should be fact or fiction?" he asked with a straight face.

"Very funny." She snapped her fingers. "My friend Tony Seton is former network news producer. He won some national awards. Now he's a writer who also edits and publishes other people's books. You'd like him. We'll meet him for coffee some time and he can tell you more."

Cody shot her an interesting look.

"What?" she asked him.

"I'm thinking that you and I should collaborate on this book."

Francie cocked her head and said, "Working together could be a real test of our relationship."

"Yes it could be," Cody said, "A test I have no doubt that we would pass with flying colors."

Francie looked at her watch. "I think we should turn around. I don't want to get you back too late. We'll stop and pick something up at Erik's. You can have it at your new desk. Don't spill."

They chattered about the book as they walked back to the car, and kept up the book talk while waiting for their food. They were still talking about it when Francie dropped Cody off at the station. He got out of the passenger side with his shoes and lunch and came around to Francie's side to say good-bye. He was about to kiss her when she stopped him with, "Cody..."

"Yes, Francie?"

"Do you think it's too soon to ask for a sabbatical?"

He answered her with their signature peck and then went into the building to report the news.

About the Author

Tony Seton is a journalist, writer, publisher, public speaker, business and political consultant, and otherwise communications specialist. Early in his career as a broadcast journalist, he covered Watergate, six elections, and five space shots, produced Barbara Walters' news interviews, and won a handful of national awards for his business-economics coverage for ABC Network Television News. Later, he wrote and produced two award-winning public television documentaries. He has conducted over 2,500 interviews and is the author of more than 2,200 essays and 20 books, and has published another dozen for clients.

Locally, Tony wrote weekly profiles for the *Carmel Pine Cone,* and restaurant reviews for the *Monterey County Weekly,* and was senior writer for *65 Degrees* magazine.

As a political consultant, Tony's clients have included Nancy Pelosi, Tom Campbell, and the American Nurses Association, as well as a ringful of local candidates.

Other hats he's worn include teacher, media trainer, and web designer.

When he's not working, he is flying, taking photographs, and walking on the beach....though even then he is often communicating, with other denizens of the dunes, both human and avian.